You get THREE
GOLD STARS

for reading
this book
(good choice).

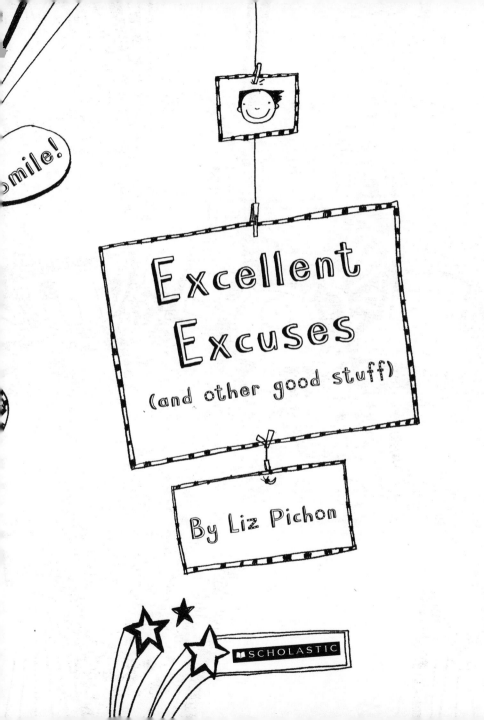

Smile!

Excellent Excuses
(and other good stuff)

By Liz Pichon

SCHOLASTIC

Published in the UK by Scholastic, 2021
Euston House, 24 Eversholt Street, London, NW1 1DB
Scholastic Ireland, 89E Lagan Road,
Dublin Industrial Estate, Glasnevin, Dublin, D11 HP5F

SCHOLASTIC and associated logos are trademarks
and/or registered trademarks of Scholastic Inc.

First published in the UK in 2011

Text & illustration © Liz Pichon Ltd, 2011

The right of Liz Pichon to be identified as the
author and illustrator of this work has been asserted by
her under the Copyright, Designs and Patents Act 1988.

ISBN 978 1407 19344 1

A CIP catalogue record for this book is available from the British Library.

Tree
photograph
Pg: 21 courtesy
of
Lily Pichon
Flannery.

Printed by CPI Group (UK) Ltd, Croydon, CR0 4YY
Paper made from wood grown in sustainable forests and other controlled sources.

13

www.scholastic.co.uk

(Homework snacks.)

Wake up this morning and suddenly remember something absolutely

BRILLIANT!

I can forget ALL about lessons (and irritating things like Marcus Meldrew). And concentrate on GOOD stuff like:

☺ Inventing {new} ways to annoy my sister Delia. (So many!)

☺ Drawing pictures (that annoy Delia). Ha! Ha!

☺ Watching TV ◉◉ and eating caramel wafers. WAFER

☺ Eating caramel wafers WAFER and watching TV. ◉◉

And most importantly...

-Band practice for

DOG ZOMBIES with Derek (who's my best mate and next-door neighbour).

Tonight we're planning a sleepover zzzzzzzz at his. Which is easy :) to do as he's so close.

Excellent choice.

OK!

One of the other "great" things about going to Derek's is he doesn't have an annoying sister (like me) ...

... AND he has a dog called Rooster.

Woof

Which I know is a stupid name for a dog, but I'm getting used to it (sort of).

Sometimes Rooster can be 'almost' as annoying as Delia. Especially when he won't stop

BARKING!

Occasionally Derek throws him a Doggy Treat to shut him up.

Yum!

But if that doesn't work, I give him a
pair of Delia's sunglasses 🔽 👓
to chew on. 🐩 It keeps him happy 😊
for HOURS.

Right now I can hear Delia 😠
shuffling around outside my
bedroom (which usually means trouble). ⚡

So I *LEAN* on my door to stop her
from barging in.

Somehow she **still** manages to
stick her **BIG** head
around the door.

She says...

(That doesn't sound good ... groan.)

I wish I could shut Delia up with a doggy treat ... how good would that be?

When I see Mum, she's holding a letter from school. I'm trying really hard to remember

ANYTHING I've done

that might have got me into trouble.

No ... can't think of anything. Nothing at all.

(I am innocent.)

But by the way Mum is looking at me, in that

What have you got to say for yourself?

kind of way, I must have forgotten something. She gives me the letter to read.

OK, just remembered.

To Mr and Mrs Gates
RE: Tom Gates Dog Attack

Dear Mr and Mrs Gates,

I do hope that Tom has recovered from the vicious dog that attacked him on the last day of term as he walked to school.

What luck that he had his schoolbook to defend himself with.

I'm SO glad it was only his homework that was chewed and not Tom. Enclosed is ANOTHER copy of the HOMEWORK – to review a film/book/TV show – for Tom to complete again during his holiday.

Let's hope there are no other **ANGRY** beasts ready to pounce in the future!

Many thanks for your help.

Kind regards

Mr Fullerman
Class 5F Form Tutor

I am trying to explain to Mum what happened to me by reenacting the **whole** scene in slow motion.

(There was no choice ... it was me or the homework.)

But she's not impressed. I think she suspects I might have made up the dog attack (I did).

Instead I have to agree to:

1. Do my review homework. (AGAIN.)

2. Not use vicious dogs as an excuse for lack of homework (or any other

kind of creature, for that matter).

3. **T**idy my room. (Mum added that one.)

Still, at
least I have

to do the
review homework in.
Though I will probably leave it until the last
possible moment, like the night before school.
That works for me.

"NOW?

What do you mean I have to do my homework right now? I've still got

TWO WHOLE WEEKS!"

Mum says, "There's no time like the present." Then she adds, "No sleepover at Derek's until you've done your homework." Which is a

DISASTER!

I have to think of something to review quickly. Mmmmmmmmm. Think ... think ... think ... think ... think...

If I don't think of something *FAST* Mum will keep me in the house

FOR EVER. Then just to add to the

PRESSURE, Derek phones up to find out what time I'm coming over for the sleepover and band practice.

when

I hear Mum saying,

That all depends on how long it takes Tom to do his review homework, Derek.

(That's ALL I need.)

Mum thinks I should go to my room to ...

"sit quietly and concentrate on getting it done".

(It's not working.)

BLANK

So I do some drawing instead.

It's a lot more fun inventing my own
characters...

Ha Ha!

THE BODGE BROTHERS

Straw?

Rubbish at EVERYTHING

The ONLY thing I can think of that I
could review is the DUDE3 concert that
Dad took me to. It's actually a BRILLIANT idea
because DUDE3 are amazing.

(Even Mr Fullerman is a fan.)

Suddenly my review will be no problem at all.
Derek's house ... here I come.

REVIEW HOMEWORK

By Tom Gates.

I went to see the DUDE3 concert.

They are the

BEST BAND IN THE WHOLE WIDE WORLD

and anyone who doesn't think so is a total IDIOT.

The End

I run downstairs and show it quickly to Mum.

There ... all done.

I am busy packing a few essentials for Derek's house when this time Dad comes up to see me.

Apparently Mum doesn't think I am taking my `review` homework "seriously". Dad says I have to do it again "PROPERLY".

Which is a bit HARSH. (OK, I admit my review was short, but true.)

Dad suddenly holds up a packet of wafers.

"For the sleepover, when you've done your homework again, OK?"

SUDDENLY I am VERY

INSPIRED.

In fact I have a TOTAL 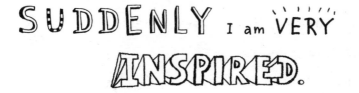 BRAIN WAVE

to get my homework done in double-quick time

(I am a genius). :)

I run d
        o
         w
          n stairs and grab

the first book from the shelf that

looks thick (but not TOO thick). Mum

sees that I am holding a BOOK and

assumes that:

TOM + THICK BOOK = SERIOUS ATTEMPT AT HOMEWORK.

(She looks pleased with me.) SIGH...

The book I've got is about ...
let me see ... ⊙ ⊙

TREES!

Never mind, that will have to do. I can see there's a lot of good stuff written on the back of this book (and inside!) that will help make my REVIEW seem very impressive indeed.

Here goes.

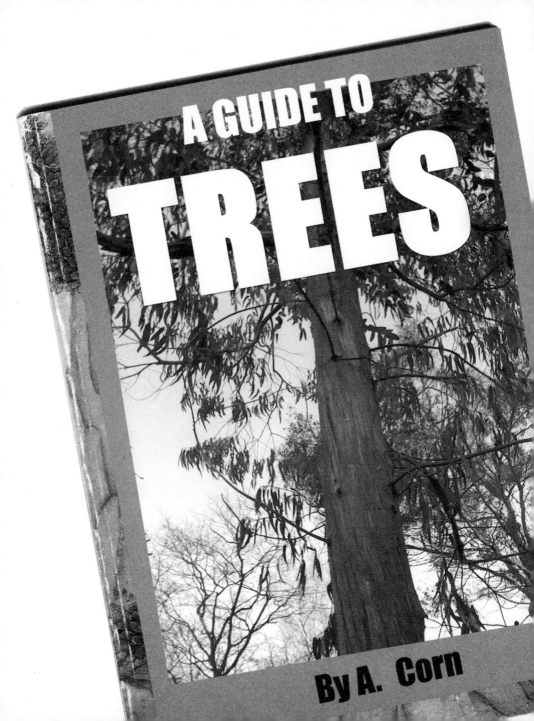

A GUIDE TO
TREES

By A. Corn

Homework FINISHED.

YEAH!

I tell Mum and Dad and they want me to
READ it to them.

"What, NOW?" 😟

"Yes, Tom, now. We'd love to hear it."

(Which actually means – just checking you've
really done it this time.)

Delia is lurking in the kitchen trying to listen. So I shut the kitchen door (in her face), then read it as ⟨⟩━━━ quickly as I can.

LUCKILY, my homework is
EXCELLENT (if I do say so myself).

Mum and Dad are pleased ☺ and slightly surprised I've managed to write **such** a good review SO quickly. I let them see it by *WAFTING* it under their noses ... super fast.

WAFT

(Must remember to hide the book on trees too.)

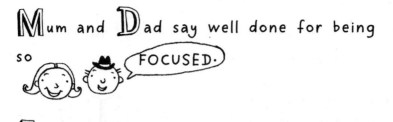

Mum and Dad say well done for being so FOCUSED.

I say, "It's all down to

GOOD PARENTING."

(Which is something I've heard my teachers say.)
Then I add, "I'm actually VERY interested in TREES." (I'm not.)

SO SWEET

This goes down really well and stops Mum and Dad from asking me any more difficult questions.

GREAT!

(I should say nice stuff like that more often.)

They are both in a good mood 🙂 now so I suggest that another sign of

GOOD PARENTING

would be to reward my hard work and EFFORT with some

EXTRA

pocket money?

Which doesn't go down quite so well...

No chance.

(Worth a try, though.)

SLEEPOVER AT DEREK'S.

Derek is happy

Yeah!

I've brought ➡ SNACKS.

But stupidly, ☹ I've forgotten to bring my

guitar 🎸 for band practice. **A**nd far
more importantly, I've left

my special teddy 🧸 at home. (I don't tell
Derek because we agreed that Special Teddies
were probably a bit **TOO** babyish now we're
in a band.)

WRONG

Luckily Derek's house is only next door to mine. So I nip back home to get them both.

Delia is sitting in the front garden with her "dodgy" boyfriend Ed (or Ted or whatever his name is). He says, All right, Tom? (Which is nice and takes me by surprise.) Then Delia shouts,

Get lost ... idiot.

(Which is not a surprise at all.)

That's when I notice Ed and Delia are actually UGH! HOLDING hands.

27

It's HORRIBLE.

I feel a bit sick and have to run into the house quickly.

I grab my guitar, teddy AND a selection of embarrassing photos of Delia that I've been saving for a VERY special occasion.

I think this might be the SPECIAL occasion I've been waiting for.

Delia with a potty on her head.

Delia after cutting her own hair with play scissors.

Delia after I pushed her into the mud (my personal favourite).

Delia with scary smile.

Delia with more bad hair and spots.

Derek can't stop laughing at Delia's OLD photos.

Ha! Ha! Ha! Ha! Ha! Ha!

We both agree that photos this funny need to be shared with OTHER people.

Other people like

Delia's boyfriend ED.

(I have a **VERY** good plan.)

We cleverly attach all the photos (plus a few extra drawings) to Derek's fishing line. Then we dangle them out of the [] just behind Delia's head.

huh?

Our plan seems to be working. **E**d is laughing a lot. Unlike Delia, who is wondering what he's laughing at.

Luckily we manage to pull up the photos before Delia works out what's going on. At least they're not holding hands any more.
SUCCESS!

(It's a good start to the sleepover.)

DOG ZOMBIES Band Practice

next. **M**r Fingle

(Derek's dad)

is hovering outside the garage where we practise. Derek says we can't start until his dad is **OUT** of the way completely.

This is because he likes to give us **tips** on music, which Derek finds **very** embarrassing. Mind you, my dad is **EXACTLY** the same. (What is it with dads and music? ♪ ♪ ♪). **M**r Fingle keeps his record collection and record player in the garage.

34

All his records are in alphabetical order and Derek says he spends HOURS cleaning them 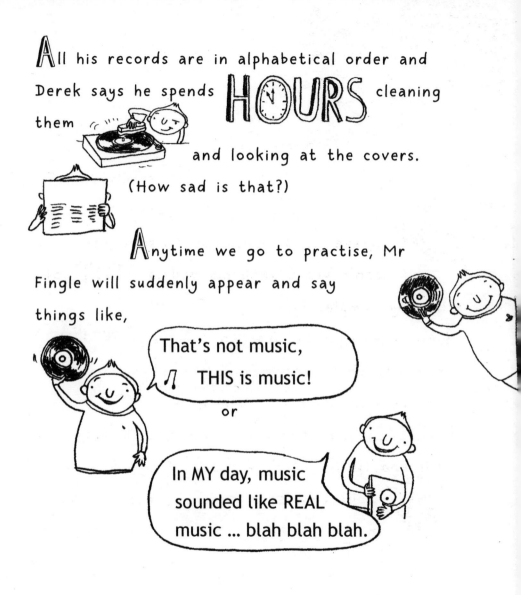 and looking at the covers. (How sad is that?)

Anytime we go to practise, Mr Fingle will suddenly appear and say things like,

That's not music, ♩ THIS is music!

or

In MY day, music sounded like REAL music ... blah blah blah.

Derek warns me...

"If my dad EVER says to you,

'*Have you heard of this band, Tom?*'

just say **YES.**

What happens if I say NO? I ask.

"You'll be forced to listen to **CRACKLY OLD** records **FOR EVER**. So trust me. Just say **YES** and pretend you know all about the band already."

OK, I agree.

He's still there.

We wait until Mr Fingle is safely out of the way before sneaking in and getting started.

If we are **EVER** going to become like **DUDE 3** (*★**BEST**★ band in the world)

we need to learn a few more songs. Which won't be easy because right now the ONLY song we can play all the way through (just about) is **DELIA'S A WEIRDO**

Which goes like this...

Delia's a Weirdo

Who's that weirdo over there?
Dressed in **bLack**
With greasy hair
You can't trust her
She's not nice
She's got no heart
Just a block of ice

CHORUS

Delia
She's a WEIRDO
Delia
She's a GEEK
Delia
She's a WEIRDO
Delia
She's a FREAK

Delia's a grumpy moo
Don't let her
Stand next to you
Big black glasses
Hide her eyes
She really smells
And that's no lie

CHORUS

Delia enjoying
the song.

Derek plays me a song called

WILD THING

(It's an oldie his dad taught him.)

It's ACE! But I think we might need
another band member to play it properly.
I don't think Derek can keep playing drums and
keyboard ...

... at the same time.

Luckily, Derek agrees.

TRIP

We are chatting about how to find a new band member when his dad suddenly appears.

TV advert

MASSIVE POSTER ✓

NEW BAND MEMBER?

I'm available!

$\mathbb{D}$erek says, "We're busy, Dad," but Mr Fingle doesn't take the hint.

"What are you playing, lads?"

"WILD THING" ... Mr Fingle,

I say. Derek gives me a "what did you say THAT for?"

look.

"'Wild Thing'. Good choice, boys. Didn't I teach you that, Derek?"

Derek's not listening. He is trying to get his dad to leave. It's not working.

"Do you know who played the original version of 'Wild Thing'?" Mr Fingle asks.

(In my head 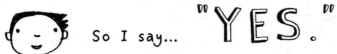 I'm thinking about what Derek told me.)

So I say... **"YES."**

Then Mr Fingle says,

"Really? Did you know the The Wild Ones recorded it in 1965, but it's **The Troggs'** version that everyone remembers."

Now it gets tricky.

Mr Fingle then asks me,

"Have you heard of **The Troggs**, Tom?"

And for a split second I forget what I'm

supposed to say (because I've said YES

already, and I don't want to be rude). I hear

myself saying,

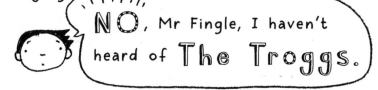

NO, Mr Fingle, I haven't heard of The Troggs.

And that's it ... he's **off!**

Looking through his record collection to play us

the original version of Wild Thing.

Derek rolls his eyes and says

we might as well leave him

to it.

Oh no...

"He won't even notice we're gone," Derek says.

He's right.

Derek and I spend the rest of the evening chit-chatting about Delia's dodgy photos ➡️ (VERY funny).

And how **BRILLIANT** it was

sneaking back to my house and sticking even MORE photos around when Delia wasn't looking!

Delia's photos + me and Derek = Genius

+ 😊 😊 = GENIUS

Mrs Worthington's moustache gets a mention too.

* ☾ *

It's getting late and I'm really tired, but I don't want to be the first one to go to sleep because I'm waiting for the right moment to bring out my teddy.

Then Derek says that

"JUST FOR TONIGHT" he's going to use

his ➡ 🐻 teddy as a [PILLOW]

because it helps him sleep. 🐻😴

And I say, "That's SUCH a good idea!" And

take my teddy 🧸 out too.

Then we eat some snacks ...
and a few more. Until we both fall
fast asleep zzzzzzzzzzzzzzzzzzzzzz
zzzzzzzzzzzzzzzzzzzzzzz

NO SCHOOL YEAH!

So far I'm having a very good holiday and **NOT** missing school at all. I'm keeping busy by doing all kinds of GOOD STUFF

like:

☺ Finding NEW places to hide

𝔻elia's sunglasses.

☺ Sleepovers at Derek's.

☺ Listening to **DUDE 3** and trying out new **ROCK STAR** poses.

☺ More drawing and doodling.

This is a good game...

Do a scribble

then see what you can turn it into.

Like ⬆ this ... ALIENS!

This game is particularly good to play in **BORING** ⊖ ⊖ lessons, as it looks like you are VERY busy.

 ← (mmm? any ideas?)

I am perfectly happy and have 🙂 LOADS of ideas for more drawings when Dad comes in and interrupts.

Are you ready?

 "What for?"

"Remember? You're staying at your cousins' for the afternoon."

"What for?"

"Because your mum and I are both working. It's just for a few hours."

"Can I go to Derek's?"

"The Fingles are out shopping today."

groan

"The

"You mean Granny and Granddad?
They're out and about too."

"I'll stay here with Delia."

"You must be desperate, Tom. She's going out.
Sorry, you have to go to your cousins'. Just
try not to do anything silly ... like last time."

(The Fossils... "out and about.")

GROAN ... looks like I don't have much choice. Then Dad adds,

"Oh, and **PLEASE** DO **NOT** mention my birthday to Uncle Kevin or Aunty Alice. I don't want any fuss this year."

Surprise!

Dad's birthday last year

"OK."

"And don't mention how many parking tickets I have ... Uncle Kevin doesn't need to know."

"OK."

There seem to be a LOT of things I'm not allowed to mention to Uncle Kevin and Aunty Alice. I sometimes don't remember them all.

parking
~~tickets~~
~~birthdays~~

Last time I was there for a visit, Uncle Kevin kept asking Dad about his job. And I heard Dad say...

"Well, I've just moved to a fantastic NEW office that is much closer to home . So I do a lot less travelling and it's far more suitable for my work." So I said...

Dad's office is in the GARDEN ... it's a shed.

Which is TRUE!

But Dad gave me one of those

"what did you have to say

that for?" stares.

I definitely don't mention the tin of biscuits he keeps in the shed because I know that's a secret.

Occasionally my cousins

play tricks on me. He He He He

Some tricks are funnier than others.
This one was annoying.

It was REALLY embarrassing when
Aunty Alice followed
the chocolate
footprints right back to me.

(One reason I don't want to go to the
cousins'.)

So I am (very slowly) getting ready to go, when Delia comes up to me and says...

"If you're going to the cousins', will you do me a favour?"

"What?"

"DON'T COME BACK ... EVER."

SUDDENLY I think of some GOOD reasons to go after all.)

1. Delia won't be there to annoy me. ☺

2. They keep LOTS of cakes and biscuits in the house.

3. There's **MASSIVE**

TVs all over the house.

4. And EXTRA **LARGE** SOFT COMFY SOFAS

How bad can it be? ☺

On the drive over, Dad is trying to remember if he has money for the parking meter.   I can tell he's a bit grumpy today.

He says,

"Don't get chocolate stuck under your shoes again..."

(That was the cousins' fault!)

"AND don't break anything that's expensive."

"Everything in their house is expensive, Uncle Kevin said so."

This cushion is very expensive.

"Did he? Well just because something is EXPENSIVE, Tom," Dad says as we drive up to Uncle Kevin's BIG house, "doesn't mean it's better, or any more ... well, TASTEFUL."

Dad is very pleased Uncle Kevin has already gone. "I can park in his space for free," he says.

Aunty Alice opens the door and tells us,

"You've just missed your Uncle Kevin!" Come in!

And Dad says,
"What a SHAME! We did try to get here earlier."

(We didn't.)

Then Dad thanks Aunty Alice for having me and promises not to be too long. BYE!

I go and find the cousins, who are busy eating snacks

 (which is a good start).

But they don't seem keen on sharing their snacks with me. Huh?

Instead we go to the food cupboard (which is STUFFED full of treats). The cousins tell me to help myself.

"You're a guest, take those biscuits ... they're nice."

Tuck in!

BRILLIANT!

(It would be rude not to.)

I manage to ➡ CRAM ⬅ LOTS

into my pockets and carry the rest in a **BIG** pile.

Which is so high I can't see ⊙ ⊙ where I'm going. The cousins help out by shouting directions.

"Forward."

"Forward."

"Keep going...

Keep going." "KEEP GOING ...
WHOOPS!"

I walk

BANG

SMACK into Aunty Alice.

 Who suggests I
put a few snacks back.
(I think the cousins have
tricked me.) I'm allowed to keep the caramel
wafers and a drink. Which is good news
because at least I get to do the "empty biscuit
wrapper" joke on the cousins...

Which they fall for

EVERY TIME.

(It's hilarious.)

When the cousins have had enough of my little

biscuit joke, I suggest we watch TV instead.

"GOOD IDEA," they say.

"Let's watch something FUNNY?"
I add. But the cousins want to watch a

SCARY film. (Which is not my idea

of fun at ALL.)
I blame ⟶ Delia. She let me

watch ⊙ ⊙

THE HOUSE WITH THE DEADLY EYES

when I was little. She thought it was funny
making me JUMP
(it wasn't).

Ha ha

But I don't tell the cousins that I REALLY don't like SCARY films.

Instead I say...

"I'll watch ANYTHING."

They choose...

VAMPIRE SWAMP MONSTERS FROM HELL

(Mmm, doesn't look too bad?)

OK, I'm wrong.

The film turns out to be <u>the</u> most

film I have EVER seen. I have to hide behind a cushion for most of it. Unlike the cousins, who can't stop LAUGHING! They think it's funny (it's not).

I can't wait until it's over.

unty Alice pops in. She says,

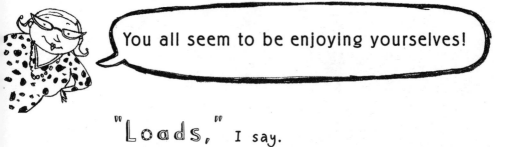 You all seem to be enjoying yourselves!

"Loads," I say.

When it's finished, the cousins suggest we watch **ANOTHER** film. (Groan.)

 "A REALLY SCARY film this time."

(What do they mean, a REALLY

SCARY one?)

Great, I'll just have to keep my eyes SHUT ⇒ ⇐ the ENTIRE time now.

They put on:

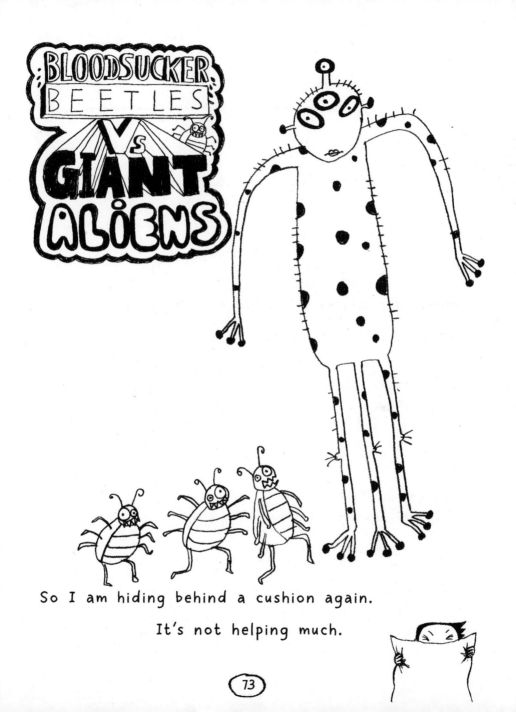

So I am hiding behind a cushion again.

It's not helping much.

I can still hear the scary stuff
through the cushion.

Luckily Dad turns up early to pick me up.

PHEW!

I AM SAVED.

Hooray
HOORAY!

In front of the cousins, though, I pretend to

be VERY sad that I won't get to see the
rest of the film. SHAME.

"Maybe next time you're round," the cousins
say to me. (I hope not.)

Aunty Alice tells Dad I've been "no trouble at all".

For some reason Dad asks, "No chocolate stains on the carpet or antiques broken, then?"

(Thanks for reminding everyone, Dad.)

"Nothing damaged. But speaking of old antiques ... isn't it your birthday soon, Frank?"

And I hear Dad say, "My birthday's not for **AGES**." Which isn't true at <u>ALL</u>. So I mention that Dad's birthday is actually NEXT WEEK. How could anyone forget their own birthday?

Aunty Alice INSISTS that we should all go out and celebrate.

"Just like last year. It will be

(Dad's birthday present last year.)

Dad doesn't seem keen on the idea. I can tell he's trying very hard to think of reasons not to go when Uncle Kevin bursts in through the door.

"Frank! I hope you paid for parking. There's a traffic warden looking at your car."

From the way Dad *RUNS* out of the door, I'm guessing he didn't buy a ticket.

We all follow him outside. Dad is **REALLY CROSS** and shouting rude things. Uncle Kevin is shaking his head in a disapproving way.

So I tell Uncle Kevin that HE'D be CROSS too if he had TEN

parking tickets like Dad.

Now Dad's cross with ME for saying how many tickets he's got.

Like it's MY FAULT!

Dad's in a REALLY bad mood all the way home. But that's NOTHING compared with how cross MUM is when she finds out that: You've done What?

1. **D**ad got **ANOTHER** parking ticket (number eleven).

2. **W**e <u>have</u> to go to dinner with the cousins for Dad's birthday.

3. **I** watched Vampire Swamp Monsters From Hell (well, sort of).

I don't think I'll be going back to the cousins' again for a while,
which means I won't be able
to watch the rest of

BLOODSUCKER BEETLES vs GIANT ALIENS.
(RESULT!)

During the night I wake up 👀 with a HORRIBLE PAIN in my 🦷 Agh! tooth. I sneak to the bathroom to take a proper look.

HOLE

It's not good. I can see a BIG black hole in it ... oh no ... groan.

I brush my teeth in the hope 🙂 that the hole will suddenly close up and go away.

It doesn't. It just HURTS even more.

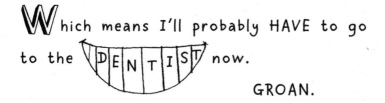

Which means I'll probably HAVE to go to the DENTIST now.

GROAN.

🍬 + 🦷 = 🙁

If Mum finds out I have a toothache she won't let me have ANY sweets or snacks for a while. And she DEFINITELY won't let me take treats over to DEREK'S house.

My treats

Snacks!

Mum's treats

Too late.

Mum must have heard me in the bathroom groaning and has woken up.

I'm poking my tooth when she knocks on the door. I tell Mum that I can't sleep because I have a headache. And I'm having "bad dreams" from watching the SCARY film at the cousins'.

Poor TOM

Mum gives me some medicine (which brilliantly stops my tooth hurting).
I go back to bed and try to get some sleep.

But in the morning my toothache

is BACK. 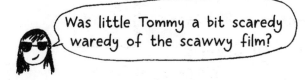 Still Here And if that's
not bad enough ...

... the first thing DELIA says to me is,

Was little Tommy a bit scaredy
waredy of the scawwy film?

GREAT ... Mum must have told her I
woke up in the night. On top of calling
me a scaredy cat, she keeps on
sneaking up behind
me and saying

which is getting on
my nerves.
So I do this drawing to cheer me up.

$\mathbb{I}$'m eating breakfast on the non-painful side of my mouth (and trying not to dribble) when Derek comes round and asks if I want to go swimming.

(Which might take my mind off this toothache.)

So I say **yes** and hope for the best. At least Delia won't be there to annoy me.

Question: What's more irritating – Delia or toothache?

Answer: Delia – because eventually toothache goes away.

MY SWIMMING Shame

I've been *groaning*

a bit due to my tooth

A THROBBING, Derek asks me

if I'm OK. I don't mention my toothache because I'm hoping the water will SOOTHE my face and make it go away completely.

AND Derek has TREATS for after swimming that he said he'd share with me. Instead I tell him that my groaning is due to Delia SHOVING me and injuring my arm. Which is true ... she did.

Derek is very glad ☺ he doesn't have a sister like me.

I'm happy with a dog.

When we get to the pool, it's pretty busy already. I spot quite a few kids from our school swimming, including ...

Amy is the smartest girl in the school, which is excellent for me as I get to take the occasional sneaky peak at her work.

The girls are too busy chatting and swimming and don't see us come in.

Derek and I decide to play it cool and only say to them if they say hello to us first.

(Good plan.)

So we go off to get changed and I'm

Rummaging around in my bag

looking for my swimming trunks.

I can't find them ANYWHERE.

I have a HORRIBLE feeling I've left them at home. (I have.)

Derek makes two suggestions:

1. I should swim in my PANTS. (That's <u>not</u> going to happen.)

2. He has a very OLD pair of trunks in his bag I can borrow.

I say, "GREAT." At least I'll be able to swim now.
Derek passes them to me under the changing room door.

When I see them, I'm wondering exactly how old these trunks really are? The teddy bear pattern makes me think Derek was probably about FOUR when he last wore them.

They are a bit short so I have to keep my towel round me until the very LAST minute. Then I quickly jump in the pool and hope no one has seen me.

Derek and I swim up and down and do some diving, which is fun. 🙂

(It makes me forget about my toothache ... well, almost.)

Amy and her friends still haven't seen us yet, but Norman Watson has. ⊙ ⊙

He's waving like from the other side of the pool. Norman's brought his little brother with him, who looks just like him only smaller. They come and join us, which is good because [now] we can all play SHARK together.

D erek is the SHARK first.

He manages to swim and catch me. Now it's

my turn to be the SHARK. YEAH! I spot

Norman (who's not great at hiding) and quickly

swim to catch him. Now Norman is the

SHARK. I've never seen Norman swim

before... So it's a bit of a surprise when he

starts to SPLASH!

He's not moving much, just ...

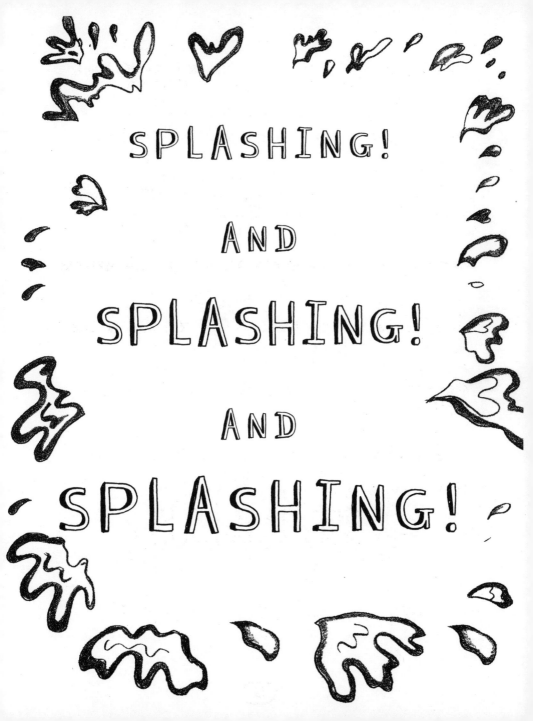

His arms and legs are thrashing around

making **MASSIVE**

waves in the pool. The splash is SO huge the

lifeguard looks over and blows her whistle.

 We're all told to:

GET OUT OF THE WATER!

The lifeguard dives in and "rescues" Norman

(who's **not** drowning, just swimming

VERY badly).

Everybody is standing at the side of the pool

watching (including Amy, Florence and Indrani).

While Norman is explaining to the lifeguard about his "unusual swimming style", the lifeguard tells us,

"No more **crazy** splashing or you'll have to get OUT!"

It's VERY embarrassing.

Then if **THAT'S** not bad enough, Amy comes over and says to me,

"Nice teddy swimming trunks, Tom."

(I'd forgotten all about my teddy-bear swimming trunks ... groan.)

And I can hear Florence and Indrani laughing.

I jump back in the pool quickly to hide.

Norman's little brother **A**lfie jumps in too
and wants to challenge me to a race.

He's only small, I don't want to hurt his
feelings ...

so I give him a head start.

RACE
YOU!

How was I supposed to know Alfie's swimming "style" was even

WORSE than Norman's?

(The lifeguard has seen enough splashing for one day.)

It was a short swim, but on the way home I realize that my toothache 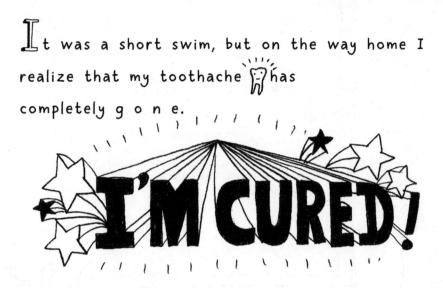 has completely g o n e.

I'M CURED!

I won't have to go to the dentist after all now.

BRILLIANT!

WATER + SPLASHING = TOOTHACHE CURE

I celebrate by taking the very small sweet that Derek offers me.

AGHHHH!

(Which is a mistake.)

LAST DAY OF HOLIDAY

Bad news is ... my tooth is still throbbing quite badly. I can't believe the holiday has gone **SO** **FAST** and I'm back at school tomorrow.

If I tell Mum about my tooth, I could probably get the day off school. But that would mean having to:

1. Go to the DENTIST.

2. **G**et stuff done to my tooth.

3. **N**ot eat **TREATS** or any sweet stuff for a very long time.

4. **C**atch up on the schoolwork I missed.

Work you missed, Tom.

Instead I |try| to forget all about my toothache by doing some drawing.

My drawings

...I'm STILL thinking

about my
TOOTHACHE.

(Groan.)

I know, I'll do a BIG ↕ poster for
DOGZOMBIES instead.

Derek and I definitely want a drummer
for the band. We can put the poster on the
school noticeboard tomorrow.
It will GRAB everyone's attention.

(That's the plan, anyway.)

That should do the trick.

(Tooth still hurting, though.)

BACK TO SCHOOL

I'm struggling to get out of bed even more than usual. (I didn't sleep so well; ⊖ ⊖ tooth still throbbing.) School starts in half an hour and I have a LOT of things to remember today, like...

☺ LUNCH

☺ MY REVIEW HOMEWORK

important → ☺ DOGZOMBIES DRUMMER POSTER ☆

☺ PE KIT

(Or I'll be forced to wear something from the SPARE KIT BOX.)

SPARE KIT BOX

I eat breakfast carefully (on the good side of my mouth.) Mum tells me to get a move on! She thinks I'm suffering from "BacktoSchoolitis".

"Very common on the first day back at school."

Delia says, "He's got

IRRITATING BROTHER SYNDROME."

(Which is annoying.)

Dad asks me, "Have you got your lunch? Got your homework?"

"Got worms?" Delia adds.

Normally I would defend myself with

a HILARIOUS and funny 😬

answer. But I think the toothache has stopped

that part of my brain from

working properly

... for now.

Funny part
of the
brain

Derek and I are a bit late for school.

We try and do fast walking while I show

Derek the

DRUMMER POSTER.

😊 He's impressed and offers to put the

poster up for me.

"You'll forget," he says.

(Harsh but true.)

Back in class, it's like we've never been away. Marcus Meldrew manages to ANNOY me within **TWO** seconds of sitting down at my desk.

He pulls up his school jumper and shows me his T-shirt.

I can't believe it!

He's wearing a special **DUDE3** T-shirt that the WHOLE band have signed!

"It's NEW and the signatures are hand-stitched on so they won't ever wash out."

"I'm ffwwilled for you, Marcus," I say.

(My tooth is throbbing, so I'm finding it hard to speak properly.)

Mr Fullerman begins to call the register and I answer,

"Earrrrr, suuurrrrr."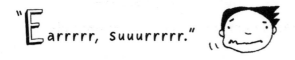

He thinks I'm trying to be funny. Ha! Ha! (I'm not!)

Then the class start laughing and Mr Fullerman peers over the register.

His beady eyes are fixed on ME.

He says,

"TOM ... I hope you've remembered your REVIEW HOMEWORK. You've had two weeks to do it. And a letter to remind you."

And I say, "Eeeerrrrrrrrrrr" (to give myself time to think).

Because I CAN'T believe I've gone and forgotten it!

What I SHOULD have said to Mr Fullerman is:

"Sorry, sir. I <u>have</u> done it, but I forgot it. I'll bring it in tomorrow."

I apologize...

But for some STUPID reason I hear myself saying:

"Sir, it's like this...
My dad got a really BAD

LURGY bug over the holidays, then we ALL got it. The doctor said it was <u>VERY</u> catching and the bugs could be \\\\\\\\\\///////////
EVERYWHERE,

including the paper I wrote my homework on.

So I just have to write it out again on **LURGY** -FREE paper just to be on the safe side.

I'll bring it in tomorrow ...

promise."

(Why, why? Why did I say that?)

Mr Fullerman says,

"Tom, is there something wrong with your mouth?"

Because this is what I *actually* said:

"Errr, it's wike thisss...

My daaa go a wearrrly add
WURGY
bug ower the
howidays, hen we AWW go it. The doctow said
it was verwy caaching and thw uggs coowld bee
EVERRWYWHERE, incwuding th aper I wwott
eye omeworwk on.

Seww I ust ave too wwitte it owwt again on
WURRGY-FWWEE apper usst to ee on the affe
ide. I'ww bwing it in ommorow ... pwomise."

I managed to mutter,

"Sore twooth, sirr ... I'm OK wrreally."

Mr Fullerman looks at me
suspiciously. He carries on
with the register but thinks I'm up to
something.

(Like I'm doing this deliberately!)

Amy and Marcus have both moved away from me because I said the word LURGY too many times.

"I have twoothache ... not the LURGY," I tell Amy.

(She might feel sorry for me.)

But she's ignoring me and staring at the classroom door.

"Tom, isn't that your dad waving at you?"

My dad? ⊙ ⊙

I look up and see someone who looks a bit like my dad?

IT IS MY DAD.

He's trying to get my attention by waving my homework around (it looks like he's swatting flies). Groan.

Now EVERYONE is STARING at him, including Mr Fullerman, who goes over to the door. He looks a bit CROSS at being disturbed.

Dad starts talking to him ... ha! ha! and they BOTH start LAUGHING.

ha!   ha!

What's SO funny?

(This is going to be embarrassing, I can feel it.)

Mr Fullerman takes my work and Dad makes a thumbs-up sign at me

(with the rest of the class still watching).

Then Mr Fullerman comes in and says in front of EVERYONE:

"Tom, your dad has very kindly dropped in your review homework. He also assures me that he's totally LURGY free and so is your homework. Which must be a HUGE relief to the WHOLE CLASS, I'm sure."

(The shame...)

At least Mr Fullerman has my homework now ...
I suppose.

I hope today gets better.
(Though it's not looking promising.)

It's no good.

My tooth is hurting so much.

I can't concentrate any more

groan.

Mr Fullerman sees that my face has

SWELLED UP

a LOT. He sends me straight to the sick room...

Not good

On the way to the sick room, I walk past some little kids who stare at me like I'm some kind of MONSTER.

E ven M rs Mumble (Oh dear, Tom.) in the school office looks concerned. She rings my (What's Tom done NOW?) dad straight away. He's only [just] got home when he has to come straight back to school.

M y tooth hurts SO badly I don't even care that he is wearing a STUPID T-shirt. Shame... Dad makes me an emergency appointment at the dentist and we drive straight there.

MY DENTIST

Most dentists try and make you feel

chilled 😊 and relaxed by having things

like fish tanks and soothing music

(to drown out the sound of

DRILLING).

But my dentist is a bit different.

He has a SCARY-looking metal crocodile

with sharp teeth on the wall. As well as

posters of people with rotten

teeth and gum diseases.

(I think he's trying to make a point.)

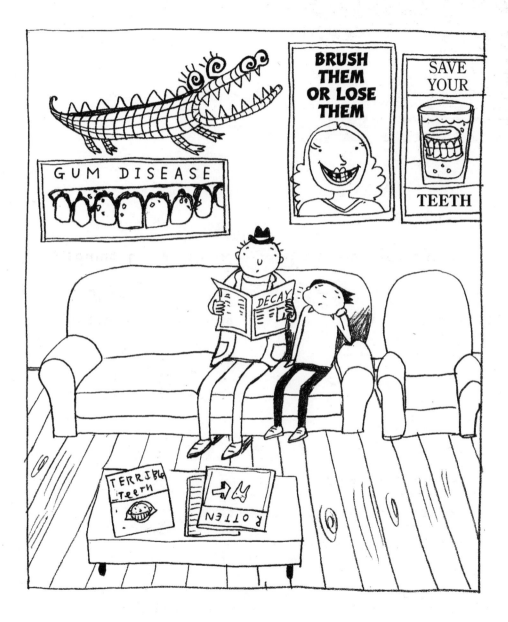

Mr Kay takes a look at me and says,

"Mmmmm, not good, young man."
(Like I don't know that already.) Then he picks at my tooth with one of those horrid metal pokey things.

"ARGH!!" I scream and he says,

"Does that hurt?"

(Errrrr, YES! LOTS!)

Apparently when I was little I once BIT a dentist.

Now Mum thinks that they have a

warning on my file like this:

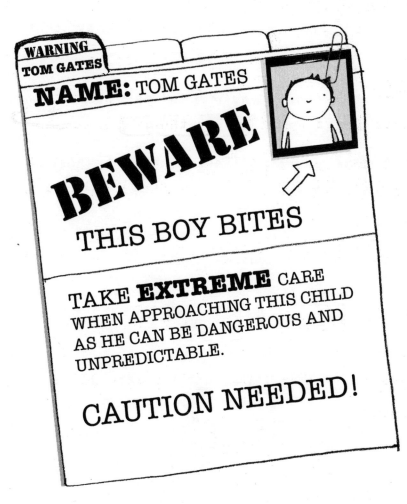

WARNING
TOM GATES

NAME: TOM GATES

BEWARE

THIS BOY BITES

TAKE **EXTREME** CARE
WHEN APPROACHING THIS CHILD
AS HE CAN BE DANGEROUS AND
UNPREDICTABLE.

CAUTION NEEDED!

Mr Kay explains EVERYTHING to me before he does it. (In case I turn vicious.)

 He says,

"Raise your hand if you feel any pain at all."

So I raise my hand ... even though he hasn't started yet.

Groan ... now he has.

I get through the injections, drilling and filling by keeping my eyes tightly ⟶ ⟵ shut and thinking of different ways of getting my own back on Delia for teasing me.

When I do open them, I can see a WEIRD mobile hanging from the ceiling.

I think it's made of teeth?

It is made of teeth.

Mr Kay points at it and says,
"That's what happens when you **don't** look after
your teeth."

It's really freaky.

I'm **SO** relieved when it's all over. ☺

My face is numb and I end up *dribbling*
the pink water Mr Kay
gives me to swish round my mouth everywhere.

Dad says I am **VERY** brave.

I agree ☺ and suggest maybe

a small **treat** might be in order?

Mr Kay suddenly remembers to give me some
"special stickers".

(They're not exactly my idea of a treat, but
I'm guessing something **SWEET** will be out
of the question now?)

Interesting selection of stickers

We stop off to pick up the tablets I have to take (I don't want my face to SWELL up again).

Dad likes my stickers. He thinks it's

HILARIOUS that my dentist is called **Mr D. Kay**...

"A dentist called Mr D. KAY – that's IRONIC," he says.
I have no idea what he's talking about.

Dad buys me a comic for a treat instead. When we get home, Mum is being
very nice to me too. Unlike Delia,   Ha!

    Ha!

who thinks it's funny to
offer me SWEETS.

Then she takes them away,
saying, "Oh, sorry, I forgot
you've just been to the
dentist. Ha! Ha!"

Mum catches Delia tormenting me and tells
her off. (Yes, Delia, back off.)

Then Mum says that I can eat my (non-chewy)
dinner on a tray in front of the telly without
Delia bothering me.

It's bliss.

After dinner Dad reminds me to take my tablet. I'm looking at the bottle and FINALLY I get Dad's dentist name joke...

Mr D. Kay.

Mr Decay.

Hilarious!

This morning Mum says I am well enough to go to school today despite me doing a "sad face". (It was worth a try.)

At least she gives me a REAL sick note that says:

Dear Mr Fullerman,
Please could Tom be excused from PE just for now as he has a nasty tooth infection which has almost cleared up.

Kind regards,
Rita GateS

But I might try and change it to ... ALL WEEK or <u>ALL MONTH</u>.
(Give it a go?)

At school, I'm busy telling a group of friends about my **DEADLY** and **DANGEROUS** tooth experience.

"It took my dentist ~~one~~ ~~two~~ ~~three~~ SEVEN WHOLE hours to save it AND the dental nurse almost *FAINTED.*"

Everyone looks impressed.

So I add, "The dentist said I was very very brave."

(That bit's true.)

Norman tells us about the time he got his head ⟹ trapped ⟸ in some railings and had to be rescued by firemen.
(Why am I not surprised?)

My mate SOLID shows us the scar on his arm from when he fell off his bike.

+++++++++++++++++++++++++++++ ↙

It looks like a long zip.

$\mathbb{D}$erek once got stuck in a cat flap (he's NEVER told me that before!).

Then Mark Clump rolls up his trousers and shows us something that looks like two dots on his leg.

"What's that?" I ask.

"Snake bite," he says. We all take a closer look.

Marcus Meldrew pretends he's not very impressed at all.

He says,

"Huh! That's nothing. I was bitten by
my new pet."

"Really? Have you got a snake too, Marcus?"
Derek asks.

"My pet is FAR more scary than a snake."

"What is it ... a man-eating

SPIDER?"   I say.

hungry

"I've got a VERY BIG new dog.

Fetch

I'm training him right now."

"A dog ... like how big a dog?"

"HUGE ... he's a bit WILD. I had to fight him off and that's when he chewed me... I've got a bad scar."

"Let's see the scar, then?" Norman asks. "No, it's still VERY painful." Marcus rubs his leg and walks away with a slight limp.

FAKE Limp

(I think Marcus is telling fibs.)

"Mind you," I say, "if I was a
dog, I'd bite Marcus too."
Derek agrees with me.

Then Mr Keen (the headmaster) blows the
whistle to go into school and
makes us J U M P.

PEEP! His face gets redder with
every puff. It looks like a
BIG RED tomato now.

PEEP!

And that's when I suddenly remember

I have a VERY good reason to:

AVOID Mr Keen.

This is because last term Mr Keen heard me singing "Delia's a Weirdo", a song I wrote about Delia.*

He immediately put me in the school concert! Which could have been **total humiliation** in front of the whole school. (Mostly due to lack of practise and slightly rude lyrics about Delia.) Luckily Derek came to my rescue and saved me from possible singing shame.

(*See p. 191, The Brilliant World of Tom Gates, for whole story.)

Mr Keen thinks I'm upset at missing the
school concert.

Oh dear. *sniff sniff*

(I'm **not**.)

I hold my bag up to my face and try to sneak
past him. Despite me using
small children for extra
cover ... he sees me.

 "TOM!"
(Keep walking, keep walking...)

**"TOM GATES! Just the person I
was looking for!"**

(Too late.)

"Yes, Mr Keen."

"I see you're in a BAND with Derek Fingle?"

(How did he know that?)

"And you're looking for a NEW drummer?"

For a TERRIBLE moment I think Mr Keen wants to join our band until he says,

"Very good poster, by the way."

Phew.

(Derek must have put the poster up yesterday.)

"I know how disappointed you were to miss out on performing in the school concert."

"No, no..."

He ignores me.

Mr Keen then tells me that Mr Sprocket

(our music teacher) has put together a

SPECIAL SCHOOL BAND

that will be performing in a very important
assembly. And GUESS WHAT? Thanks to Mr
Keen, Derek and I are IN the school band NOW.

"Isn't that exciting, Tom?"

I'm lost for words.

**"What instrument does Derek play,
Tom?"**

"Keyboards, Mr Keen ... but I don't think—"
Too late – Mr Keen has already gone.
Derek won't be happy.

Oh no...

I don't even know what kind of music the school band plays.

I suppose it might be OK? (Extra band practice for DOGZOMBIES at least.)

But Mr Keen has reminded me about the BAND AUDITION POSTER

I can't wait to find out WHO wants to be in our band!

On the way to class I go and take a quick look at the poster.

Mmmmmmmmmmm.

(Oh...)

I'm not sure everyone is taking this very
seriously.

Hang on ...
AMY PORTER

has added her name!

That's a surprise.

Amy is obviously taking DOGZOMBIES
very seriously. Because she is super smart with
excellent taste in music. I'll tell Derek the
news like this:

"YEAH! GOOD NEWS! ☺

Amy Porter is auditioning for the band.
BOO! BAD NEWS. ☹

Mr Keen has put US in the SCHOOL BAND."
(I'll say the bad news bit really fast ... he
might not notice.)

In class, Mr Fullerman asks about my tooth.

How's your tooth, Tom?

So I hand over my →REAL← sick note...

Dear Mr Fullerman,

Please could Tom be excused from PE just for ~~much~~ the week as he has a VERY SERIOUS nasty tooth

infection which has almost cleared up.

Kind regards,

Rita Gates

Mr Fullerman reads it carefully.

(I hope he doesn't spot my "changes".)

So far so good.

Then he gives me a LONG ⟶
list of work 👀 to catch up on.

I tell Mr Fullerman this MUST be a mistake
because I was only away for one day. Amy
says, "You missed loads."

Great.

Now I'm wondering if this is a good time ☺
to mention the DOGZOMBIES audition poster
that Amy signed up for. I could give her a few
tips?

(Like "Bring caramel wafers".)

But Mr Fullerman interrupts. He tells us about the **"really exciting school field trip I have planned"**.

(Sounds like fun.)

"We'll be looking out for all kinds of plants, bugs and odd creatures!"

I nudge Amy and point to Marcus...

"Found one."

Odd Creature

Forgetting that Mr Fullerman has **SUPER HUMAN** HEARING.

He gives me a teacher stare and says,

"TOM, along with finding odd creatures, I'll be expecting YOU to tell us LOTS of interesting information about trees, as it seems you're a bit of an expert."

Which shuts me up.

I have NO idea why Mr Fullerman thinks I'm an expert on trees.

A BISCUIT TREE

THIS would be my idea of an INTERESTING TREE.

Next Mr Fullerman hands out more
homework ... groan.

Class 5F Homework
From: Mr Fullerman
Oakfield School

Dear Class 5F

This week I want you to write a proper
thank-you letter.
You need to decide who you're writing to
and what you are thanking them for.
Was it a present or perhaps some good
advice?
Use your imagination.
Describe how you feel and remember to lay
out the letter correctly.
Looking forward to reading your letters.
Kind regards

Mr Fullerman

The homework could be worse, I suppose. At least it's **not** fractions or anything really tricky like that.

How hard is it to say

THANK YOU?

Unless it's to Delia.

But that NEVER happens.

At home time Derek and I are busy discussing Who has signed our DOGZOMBIES audition poster.

So far it's only Amy,

Florence

and

NORMAN.

I'm guessing SUPERMAN

and MiCKeY MOUSE

won't turn up.

I remember to tell Derek that Mr Keen might want to talk to him about being in the school band.

"I 'll just say NO thanks, Sir."

"Too Late ... we're in the school band."

"At least he doesn't know I play keyboard," Derek says.

"...he might now.

(It just slipped out, sorry.)"

Derek is wondering what exactly Mr Keen is planning, when Marcus runs past

REALLY f a s t.

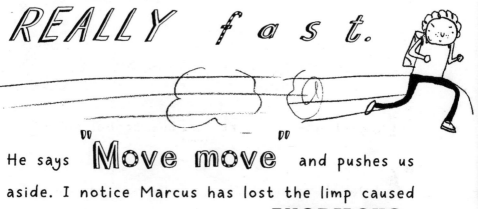

He says "Move move" and pushes us aside. I notice Marcus has lost the limp caused by the terrible SCAR from his **ENORMOUS** new dog.

"What's the hurry?" I say, but he's already gone.

Derek says, "Let's follow him outside and see what he's up to."

"OK."

Marcus has ——rushed over to his dad, who's in the car waiting. We watch Marcus open the door and *lean* inside, like he's trying to reach something.

Here, boy.

Derek says, "I can hear BARKING!"

"So can I."

"**It** <u>must</u> be his new dog!"

"**T**he one that BIT him!" I say.

Grrr

We can't see 👀 the dog yet but his BARK
is VERY **LOUD**.

Marcus is holding a dog lead and being pulled
around.

"Maybe Marcus has a **FIERCE** dog
after all?" Derek says.

"From the way he's struggling to control it, his
dog must be really **BIG**

and **STRONG**," I say...

...or maybe not.

Grrrrrrrrrr

HOMEWORK

Ever since **Mr Fullerman** sent that letter home about my **ReVIEW HOMEWORK**, Mum is being tough on me.

> Homework first, dinner after, Tom.

But it's difficult to concentrate because I keep thinking about:

1. Marcus being dragged along by

his teeny weeny dog. **Hilarious!**

2. Dinner.
3. Dinner.
4. The DOGZOMBIE drummer auditions.

It's excellent news that Amy Porter has put
her name down. She's so SUPER SMART at
EVERYTHING. I can't wait to see how good she
is at drumming.

I think this

could work.

We are holding the auditions
in Derek's garage at the weekend.
Derek's dad, Mr Fingle, has been BANNED.

NO RECORD
PLAYING ALLOWED!

Everyone who turns up will have a chance to audition, even if they're rubbish.

As well as the audition, I'm ALSO thinking about...

5. Dad's birthday, which is <u>really</u> soon. What to get him?

 -Draw a picture?

-Chocolates?

 -Socks

- New hat?

Mum told Aunty Alice

that she had

already arranged
a little get-together

for Dad to avoid having a party
like last year.

surprise

Now EVERYONE is coming round to ours.
Including Granny and Granddad Gates,
or   as I like to call them,

THE FOSSILS

because they are very
old and ancient.

Which has just given me a   GREAT idea
for my THANK YOU letter homework. Genius ...
thanks, Fossils.

TO: GRANNY GATES

Dear Granny,
THANK
YOU
FOR THE
POCKET
MONEY.
Love, Tom
(YOUR FAVOURITE GRANDSON.) x x

Tom,

I have no doubt you are a wonderful grandson.

But I need to see a much longer thank-you letter next time, please.

1 merit.

But well done for joining the NEW SCHOOL BAND. Mr Keen was extremely pleased.

Mr Fullerman

Great, now it's official.

Written in black and white by
Mr Fullerman that I AM
in the school band.

I'm guessing he wasn't impressed with my
letter.

And I only got one merit. Which is
a bit **harsh**, I think?

Maybe this might help...

To: Mr Fullerman

Let me explain about the slightly small
thank-you letter.
My granny is VERY OLD with dodgy
eyes ⊙ ⊙ and she falls asleep a lot.
So a thank-you letter needs to be in
REALLY BIG WRITING and

VERY VERY SHORT. Or she can't read
it. (I am a thoughtful grandson ...
it's true.) ☺

From: Tom Gates
        ↖(Hard-working pupil who
deserves a few more merits, maybe?)

Space left for EXTRA
merits ... is still empty.
Oh well, worth a try.

Over the next few days Mr Fullerman reminds everyone in class that...

"REALLY hard-working pupils get the extra merits."

(OK, point taken.)

So I'm doing some EXTRA reading at home when Granny and Granddad pop in for a cup of tea.

I can hear them chit-chatting

chit

chat

downstairs with Dad.

I go to say hello (and sneak a biscuit).

Tea + Fossils = BISCUITS

But Dad spots me and says, "No biscuits for you until your tooth infection has cleared up."

Just then Delia comes in and hears
the word "INFECTION".
"Ugh ... disgusting. What's he got now?"
Delia is leaning away from me like
I have THE LURGY while helping
herself to a biscuit. Right in
front of me, too!

"That's not FAIR,"
    I say.

"Delia hasn't got a bad tooth like you,"
Dad says.

"Ugh, he's Rotting," she

    laughs, holding her nose.

Granddad says that I **MUST** take care of my teeth or 😬 I'll end up looking like him. ➡️ 😟

Then he says, "Do you want to see what happens to you if you DON'T look after your teeth?"

Granny tries to stop him.

👵 "Don't show him, **Bob**... It's not nice."

Now I'm *REALLY* curious.

"Your teeth look fine to me, Granddad."

That's when he turns his back ...

and takes his teeth **OUT** of
his mouth!

It's HILARIOUS!

Now he's got them IN HIS HAND. (OK, that
looks weird.)

"See ... no teeeffff leffft."
Granddad's mouth reminds me of a very old
turtle.

Delia says, "...that's rank."
Granny tells Granddad to put them back and
"don't be so childish."

176

Which doesn't stop Granddad from
pretending to BITE Granny
before slipping his teeth back
into his mouth. (They make a
strange clunking sound as they settle down.)

 CLUNK!

Granny tries to change the subject
(well, sort of).

She's MADE her | own | biscuits.

Uh oh.

"**T**hey are **packed** full of nuts, honey and all kinds of other LOVELY stuff," she says.

Granny Mavis has very weird taste in food. So "other lovely stuff" could really be ANYTHING.

Here are a couple of her favourite "specials".

La La
La

Granny's cheese and jam sandwiches?

CHOC ← Why?

Grated chocolate on pasta...

Dad says I'm allowed a home-made biscuit if I promise to brush my teeth afterwards.

Granny arranges her "biscuits" on a plate and says, "Tuck in!"

But her biscuits look a bit like...

FISH?

(Oh dear.)

"They're not fish flavoured!" Granny assures me.

Phew. But they do have **BIG** stary eyes.
(I risk it ... for a biscuit.)

Mmmmmm, surprisingly tasty for a fish biscuit.
The eyes are a bit crunchy, though.

Delia's already left (after Granddad's teeth trick) so there are more biscuits for me. When Dad's not looking I sneak a couple for later.

RESULT!

While the Fossils are still here, Mum remembers to invite them to Dad's birthday party.

Dad is still not keen on having a party at
ALL after last year.

I did it MY way

So while he's grumbling and complaining, I
remind everyone that it's MY birthday soon.
And I'm VERY keen to have a

PARTY with presents.

Granddad wonders what I'm interested in these
days.
(Perfect time to drop "present hints".)

I am about to say **DUDE 3** electric
guitars, drawing stuff, that kind of thing.

When Mum **BUTTS** in with
"Tom's REALLY interested in trees,
aren't you, Tom?"
I am?

"Remember the wonderful
piece of homework you did
on trees?"

Errrrrrrr.

I decide to take the praise while it's being
handed to me because:

Good schoolwork + Birthday = Extra good presents

But just in case I say...

" 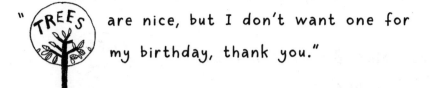 are nice, but I don't want one for
my birthday, thank you."

Granddad asks me about too.

(I'm very impressed he remembered
my band's name!)

He says he has the PERFECT venue for
us to play our VERY FIRST GIG ... when we're
ready.

"This place is always looking for new acts,"
Granddad says.

"Really?"

"Yes, you'll have a big audience of friendly people."

W☺W, EXCELLENT! I can't wait to tell Derek. Then Granny offers me another biscuit, so I take it (to go with the other two I already have).
I have LOTS of good stuff to chat about with Derek now.

☺ FIRST EVER **DOGZOMBIES** GIG

☺ FISH BISCUITS

☺ GRANDDAD'S TEETH

R ound at Derek's house, he is

STILL not very happy about

being in the school band.

S o I give him the TWO fish biscuits, which

makes him laugh.

"Your granny's weird," he says, looking at the

biscuit ⊙ ⊙ eyes.

"But they taste nice, though," he adds.   ☺

I'm telling Derek how THE FOSSILS are not

always that bonkers

and sometimes

they're REALLY funny.

"M ostly they are just like really ordinary

grandparents, honestly."

Derek says, "Are you sure about that?"

OK, maybe Derek has a point.

Mr Fullerman

... is doing that teacher thing of *leaning* on his desk Staring at everyone.

He says he has got some very IMPORTANT news for us all.

(His idea of what's important is different to mine.)

For instance ... **DOGZOMBIES** band auditions are important. I'm still not sure if I should say anything to **AMY** about them. I decide not to.

Not the right time. I notice that she's holding her pencil and tapping it on the desk (which is the sort of thing a drummer would do).

 It's **a good** sign.
☺

While I have been studying **AMY'S** drumming, Mr Fullerman has gone ahead and made his

"IMPORTANT ANNOUNCEMENT".

I've missed it. Oh well.

But then he asks me a question.

"Isn't that right ... Tom?"

(This is why I prefer being at the

BACK of the classroom, not at the front.)

I have **NO** idea what Mr Fullerman is talking about, so I just agree with him.

Yes, Mr Fullerman.

"Great, well done Tom. Does anyone else want to go too?"

Huh?

"No ... OK, looks like it's just you, Tom. And Derek too. Off you go. You'll be the first on the chart."

WHAT? THE FIRST? I have a horrible feeling about this. Well, at least I get to miss a lesson (I think?).

GOLD STAR AWARD CHART
CLASS 5F

MARK CLUMP	ROSS WHITE
BRAD GALLOWAY	SOLOMAN STEWART
TOM GATES	PANSY BENNET
PAUL JOLLY	INDRANI HINDLE
LEROY LEWIS	FLORENCE MITCHELL
MARCUS MELDREW	JULIA MORTON
TREVOR PETERS	AMY PORTER
NORMAN WATSON	AMBER TULLEY GREEN

The GOOD NEWS is, I've got the

FIRST GOLD STAR on the new

Award Chart. Mr Fullerman has given me a star for joining the school band. (Like I had a choice?)

Which is unexpected but nice.

The BAD news is, school band practice is on NOW and I have to go on my own. 😦 Oh well, at least I'm missing maths lessons in class.

Question: How bad can a school band really be?

Answer: Worse than I thought.

Mr Sprocket is delighted to see us.

Derek and I are | not | so delighted.

"Let me explain," Mr Sprocket tells us. "This school band is different. We use recycled rubbish made into instruments.

We play new modern music too."

(Which just means no one has ever heard of
it.)
"Not exactly DOGZOMBIES, is it?" I whisper to
Derek.

Parr

Mr Sprocket asks us to choose an "instrument". As there are NO guitars or keyboards I pick the plastic-bottle-looking thing with chopsticks. Derek goes for the wooden box with elastic bands.

We do the best we can under the circumstances.

When I hit the bottles they are supposed to make different notes.

So far, mine only have two notes.

CLANG! and even LOUDER CLANG!

The other kids are more practised than us - they are making it look easy (it's not!).

We keep making mistakes.

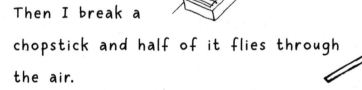

I hit the bottles too hard.

Derek has pinged quite a few of his elastic bands. PING

Then I break a chopstick and half of it flies through the air.

School band is not going well.

Even Mr Sprocket looks a little weary.

One kid puts his hand up.

"Sir, why are they in our band?"

"OUR BAND"? I thought it was a school

band?

Mr Sprocket tells him to put his hand down

because we'll be fine,

after one or two more rehearsals.

"More like one or two HUNDRED."

 Ha! Ha! Ha!

I can hear more kids laughing now.

I'm going to HAVE to think of a really

EXCELLENT excuse to get out of this band.

It's been an Awful practice.

$\mathbb{D}$erek agrees. "That was embarrassing," he says.

Then I notice where the other half of my chopstick has landed.
I nudge Derek. "No, THAT'S embarrassing."
Mr Sprocket looks like he has a bow in his hair.
We leave quickly, before he notices.

Whoops

Outside the classroom, Amy and Florence are walking past.
"Is this your new band, Tom?" Amy asks.
"No way," I say. "This is the school band. It's a bit rubbish, really." The kids in the school band hear me and are not happy.

"We're not rubbish. YOU'RE the one who's rubbish."

"And so's your friend."

"We'd be ten times better if you weren't in the school band."
(They have a point.)

GREAT. Now Amy and Florence think that we're hopeless. I'm just about to EXPLAIN to them that we play

REAL instruments in **DOGZOMBIES**

But Amy and Florence have gone.

"This **school band** could RUIN our

reputation ... if we had one," Derek says.

It's true.

Today we've been a bit:

⇨ RUBBISH

⇨ SHAMED

and ⟹ EMBARRASSED.

Derek and I decide we have to get out of

the school band, one way or another.

It's the most important thing to do ever.

Until I find a spare wafer in my pocket.

Share a
wafer?   YES

YEAH!

The poster has been up for a few days and we're doing the auditions TOMORROW, so I am very excited to see who else has added their names to the list.

Let me see...

HANG ON!

Amy Porter

AND

FLORENCE MITCHELL'S

names have been CROSSED OUT?

What's going on? Who's done that?
So far the only *REAL* person who's coming to
the audition is: HYPERACTIVE

NORMAN WATSON.

I take down the poster and go and find Amy
quickly.

Stan the school caretaker is holding open
the door for some kids. I can see ☉ ☉ Amy
and Florence in front of me. So I
RUSH past everyone, saying,

"EMERGENCY!

EMERGENCY!

EMERGENCY!"

Which gets their attention.

I catch up with Amy and Florence and show them the poster.

"LOOK at what SOMEBODY HAS done! Can you believe they've actually CROSSED BOTH your names OFF from the audition! What kind of an IDIOT would ruin your chances of being in DOGZOMBIES by doing something as STUPID as that ?"

Then Amy says,

205

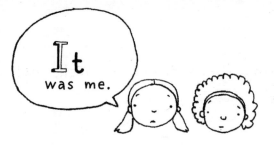

was me.

(Oh ... I wasn't expecting that.)

Florence says, "We don't play drums, Tom."

"And we didn't write our names on your poster. Sorry," Amy adds.

"Does that mean you won't be auditioning, then?" Just checking.

Caretaker Stan is listening to our conversation.

"**H**ey! Looking for a drummer? Well, look
no further!"

Stan thinks he's funny. Groan.
He pretends to do a drum
roll and cymbal crash.
(Which is rubbish.)

The door slowly closes while
Stan continues to air drum.
I'm trying not to look fed up.

"**Y**ou wouldn't want us in your band, Tom,"
Florence says.

"**W**e'd be ROTTEN," Amy adds.
"Worse than Stan?" I say.
(We can still hear Stan's keys jangling in the
background.)

Amy suspects whoever wrote the Silly names on the poster also wrote their names on it too.

Good point.

"See if you can match the handwriting on the poster to anyone in our class," Amy suggests.

"That's genius!" I say. (She's so smart.)

Whoever wanted to mess up the audition poster is probably feeling pretty pleased with themselves right now.

I'm searching the classroom for ANYONE who seems slightly more smug than usual...

mmmmm

Extreme close up

Surprise, surprise...

ENGLISH

It **WAS** Marcus who wrote on the poster. He admits it.

He says, "You didn't actually think Amy and Florence wanted to be in your band, did you?" Ha! Ha! Ha! he laughs. (He's so annoying.)

Mr Fullerman has marked all our REVIEW homework and is handing them back to us.

"Well done, Tom, excellent work," he says.

Marcus doesn't get a mention.

☺

(I did my homework quickly, so this is very good news.)

Good work, Tom.

Your special interest in trees will be very useful on the field trip.

Well Done

3 merits and ONE GOLD STAR.

THAT'S why Mr Fullerman thought I was interested in TREES.

I'll show this to Mum and Dad, who might give me a REWARD.

Cake

REWARD

REWARD

BISCUITS

CHOCOLATE REWARD

FIZZY REWARD

Cash Reward

I could try the "good parenting" line again?

Worth a go... ☺

Right now I enjoy collecting my

SECOND GOLD ⭐

2 merits = 1 GOLD STAR.

Whoever gets the MOST stars at the end of the term wins "spectacular prizes". (So Mr Fullerman tells us.)

I suspect the prizes will be things like pencil cases and school tea towels.

OAKFIELD SCHOOL

NOT very spectacular at all.

But as I am in the lead with two stars ... I don't care.

I leave my book open so MARCUS can see my

MERITS AND GOLD STARS

Sadly, nobody else (REAL) has put their names down for our audition.
Looks like it's ONLY NORMAN coming now. I don't think his audition will take too long.

Derek hopes someone else will turn up ... other than just his dad. Who keeps popping in.

Anyone here yet?

Derek sends him away.

I remind Derek that my granddad has

already booked **DOGZOMBIES'** FIRST EVER GIG!

"We can still do it, even if we don't have a drummer," I say.

(That's plan B, in case no one turns up.)

"Granddad says we'll be in front of a nice friendly crowd."

"BRILLIANT." Derek is trying to be positive.

"We could become the NEXT

DUDE 3," I say. How cool would
that be?

Then Norman turns up, which brings us right
back down to earth.

He's being his usual TWITCHY self.
"Hey, Norman, just relax and play anything you
want to," I tell him.

Whoops!

(We're not expecting too much
from him.)

"Bit nervous," he says as
he knocks over another drum.

It's not a great start.

The noise gives Derek's dad an excuse to COME in AGAIN to see what we're getting up to (like he doesn't already know).

Need any help?

I'm really hoping that Norman's drumming is better than his swimming ... but so far, it's not looking good.

Norman settles down (a bit).

Then he starts to play.

And we're all in for a MASSIVE SURPRISE...

NORMAN is AMAZING!

OK, he is a bit wild...

When he's finished playing, we tell Norman he's "IN THE BAND!" Which sets him off again.

Norman is much better at playing than we are. "We might have to practise more,"

I say to Derek.

"You'll sound like a proper band with Norman drumming!" Mr Fingle tells us.

Then he adds...

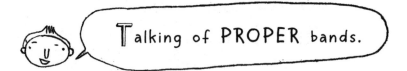

Talking of **PROPER** bands.

(Uh oh.) We haven't had a chance to

WARN Norman about

Mr Fingle's little

CHATS.

He's already rummaging in his record collection.

"Have you ever heard of a band called

THE WHO, Norman?"

"Who?" Norman says.

"NO, THE WHO,"

Mr Fingle repeats.

Then Norman asks, "Who are The Who, then?"

Which is really confusing.

Derek wants his dad to STOP chatting.

"Not now, Dad, PLEASE!"

(But it's too late.)

"Only one of the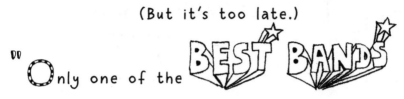

in the whole world ever!" he says as he proudly

shows Norman the record.

"This is a CLASSIC,

you must listen to it ...

right NOW!"

Norman says, "OK, sure!"

Then jumps up just a little bit too quickly to

take a look at the album.

The record flies HIGH in the air, out of its sleeve, then lands on the ground.

It rolls across the floor,

spins a bit, then

comes to a stop.

through some... dust,

Mr Fingle is FREAKING out that his record has been SCRATCHED and ruined.

"Don't PANIC,

I'll FETCH IT!" he shouts.

Really REALLY LOUDLY.

SO loudly that Rooster (Derek's dog) hears the word FETCH and

runs in from the

garden. He grabs the record in his teeth, then disappears out of the door. Followed quickly by Mr Fingle.

erek says he's never
seen his dad run so fast.

"It must be a really good album," Norman says.

"And Rooster has very good taste in music," I add.

The audition is over now, so we watch Mr Fingle chase Rooster all around the house.

When I get home,
this letter from my school
has turned up.

From: Oakfield School

To: Mr and Mrs Gates
24 Castle St
EGP 1963

I'm wondering WHAT I've done NOW? So I open
it carefully and take a sneaky look. ☉ ☉

PHEW! Just a reminder about the
school field trip and a
special ➡ <u>Clothes List.</u>

(Nothing important, then.)

I'm LATE

for the field trip due to:

1. Forgetting about the field trip.

2. Forgetting I still had my pyjama bottoms on as I left for school. I run back to get changed.

Delia sees me and is her usual helpful self.

FOOL.

I only just make it to school on time.

LATE AGAIN, TOM? Mr Fullerman and the whole class are waiting for me outside. For some strange reason Mr Fullerman is dressed like a jungle explorer?

Solid is there and wearing very impressive waterproof boots.

I ask him if Mr Fullerman is looking for BUGS or TIGERS?

He laughs **loudly** and Mr Fullerman STARES at me ... then at my feet. (Uh oh.)

Apparently I'm wearing

Inappropriate footwear

And I might have to wear the

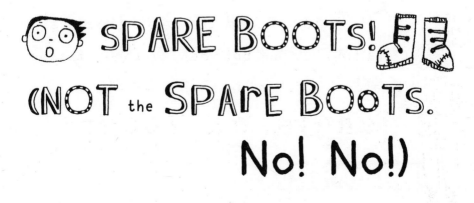

SPARE BOOTS! (NOT the SPARE BOOTS. No! No!)

The "SPARE" stuff is mostly MANKY bits of lost property that no one wants (like this).

Spare T-shirt.

Spare shorts.

(I hope he forgets about my shoes.)

MRS Mumble is on the trip with us. She's holding the bag of "spare stuff".

"For emergencies," she tells me cheerily.

"Or people with inappropriate footwear," Marcus adds.

I ignore him.

Norman is still very overexcited about being in DOGZOMBIES.

He keeps jumping around and using his magnifying glass to **LOOM** up to people with one big EYE. (It's getting on everyone's nerves.)

Marcus is getting on my nerves. "Didn't you read the field trip clothes list?" he asks me. "SHHHHH," I say.

It will be ALL Marcus's fault if I have to wear the SPARE BOOTS.

Mr Fullerman gets distracted when Norman looms up to Julia Morton once too often.

AGH!

We all have to "PAY ATTENTION" to the safety talk about things that could

STING

and

BITE.

"You must behave SENSIBLY."

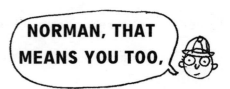

NORMAN, THAT MEANS YOU TOO,

Mr Fullerman says.

We set off with Mr Fullerman at the front and Mrs Mumble at the back to make sure no one dawdles behind.

Don't dawdle

We're not going far, just to the local field.

When we get there we are put into groups and have to go off and identify as many different types of plants, leaves and TREES as we can.

"You should be good at this, Tom, you know a lot about trees," Mr Fullerman says.

Great, now my group think I'm some kind of WEIRD TREE EXPERT (I'm not).

Instead I just make stuff up, which seems to work.

Here we have the lesser spotted tree.

I'm really looking forward to using the BUG CATCHERS we've been given.

Pansy Bennet has already found an

ENORMOUS spider.

Leroy Lewis is studying a bug that

ROLLS up in a ball.

Mark Clump is catching EVERYTHING.

Ants, bugs, spiders, frogs - the lot.

I spot a really brightly coloured beetle. I've never seen one like that before.

CLOSE UP!

I sneak up really slowly. THIS bug looks AMAZING, I might even get THREE merits (and one GOLD ☆) for discovering it.

I lower my bug catcher over the bug carefully...

Easy does it...

Marcus suddenly

traps it in HIS bug catcher.

"THAT'S MINE," he says.

(I really hope it bites him or stings him ... or both.)

Irritating or what?

Florence and Amy come over
to show me what they have found.
GRASSHOPPERS, which are very cool.
(It takes my mind off Marcus.)

Amy wonders how the audition

went "with ONLY Norman turning up?"

"He was BRILLIANT," I say.

"Really?" Florence doesn't sound convinced.

"Aren't you worried about Norman being in the band?" Amy asks.

"No, not really," I say. "Norman can be a bit, you know..."

"Bonkers," Florence adds.

So I tell them.

"You'd be surprised. Norman's actually a REALLY GREAT drummer."

"What about all the crazy things he does?" Amy says.

"Norman's not THAT bad. Honestly, when was the last time you saw him do something REALLY silly?" I add.

Just as Norman turns up holding

TWO green caterpillars

under his nose.

"LOOK ...
BOgEYS!"

(Not now, Norman ... groan.)

We are sitting on the grass eating our packed lunches when SOLID (who looks a bit miserable) shows me the only thing he's found so far.

I think 😐 😐 it's half a dead bug ...
it [is] half a dead bug.

half bug

"I'll help you find something else,"
I say.

So Solid *FLICKS* the dead bug away.

(Which probably wasn't the best idea.)

The bug flies through the air and lands right on Julia Morton's sandwich.

Julia SCREAMS and says she feels sick now.

Mrs Mumble assures her that the bug probably fell from the tree.

(Me and Solid keep quiet.)

Unlike MARCUS, who tells Julia that there is a very good reason she has only HALF a dead bug on her sandwich.

"What's that, then?" Julia asks.

"You must have EATEN the other half already."

The whole class go "UGGGGHHHHHHHhh!"

Julia turns green. (She's the same colour as the grass now.)

Marcus is laughing and being particularly irritating today.

Mr Fullerman tells everyone to "Calm down!"

He lets Julia "recover" by sitting under a tree. Then takes the rest of the class down to the pond to carry on looking for creatures.

OK, now I see why I needed to wear boots. SOLID has already SUNK down into the mud

and has to be pulled out by Mrs Mumble. (Who's a LOT stronger than she looks.) ◑ ◑

Mrs Mumble tells me to keep clear of the mud "in those shoes".

Then Marcus adds

"He should be wearing the

SPARE BOOTS,

Mrs Mumble."

SHUT UP, MARCUS! I wish he'd sink down in the mud.

Mr Fullerman calls us all over to see what he's been collecting in the bucket. Amongst all the SLIME and WEEDS are some tiny little 🐟 and other interesting things.

"Take turns to look ... don't push," Mr Fullerman says.

(Marcus is pushing now.) It's tricky to see exactly what's in there. SOLID thinks he

saw a 🐍 "WATER SNAKE!"

"You can all see ... be patient," Mr Fullerman tells us.
Then he asks Mark Clump and Amber Tulley Green to help carry the bucket up the grass.

Norman's `not` great at being patient and can't wait. He hears Solid say "WATER SNAKE" and gets really excited. Then accidentally *T R I P S* over a twig and falls on Amber.

Who lets go of the bucket.
Mark Clump holds on with one hand.
Until a BIG FROG

POPS out of his pocket. (He'd forgotten about the frog.)

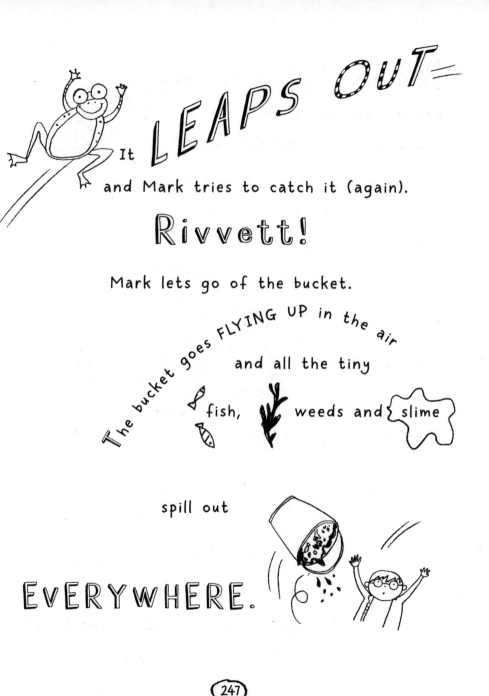

It *LEAPS OUT*
and Mark tries to catch it (again).

Rivvett!

Mark lets go of the bucket.

The bucket goes FLYING UP in the air
and all the tiny

fish,   weeds and slime

spill out

EVERYWHERE.

ALL OVER **MARCUS.**

(Turns out there wasn't a water snake in the bucket after all. Just lots and lots of slime.) Marcus is not happy. Solid has cheered up, though. Mrs Mumble comes to the rescue with a towel. She says:

"Don't panic, I've got just the thing for this kind of

EMERGENCY."

Mr Fullerman and the rest of the class scoop up any fish or creatures from the ground and take them back to the pond, while Mrs Mumble helps Marcus.

She says...

"Thank GOODNESS we brought the SPARE
CLOTHES ...

and the SPARE BOOTS!"

(I agree.)

Marcus has to wear them all the way back

to school. Which **inspires** me to draw some of the bugs and creatures I COULD HAVE found on the field trip.

Worth at least five merits, I think?

Dad's Birthday

Everyone's coming to our house for Dad's birthday party, which means Mum is a LOT more stressed than usual. She keeps saying things like

"Take it upstairs!" and

"Rubbish outside!"

Delia thinks it's funny to try and put ME outside.

Mum gets CROSS

and says that we had **BOTH** better behave

when guests arrive

or else!

The whole house is all

CLEAN and TIDY.

Until the Fingles turn up early

with their dog Rooster.

He's got really muddy paws.

Garden!

Rooster isn't in the house

for very long thanks to

Mum.

Derek gives Dad his present. (I can guess what it is from its shape.) ☺

Dad's DELIGHTED. He's already discussing with Mr Fingle "classic albums" and "great bands of our day".

(Yawn.)

It's not biscuits.

I give Dad my present before he gets too carried away chatting.

It's a T-shirt with my drawing on the front.

TOM GATES

Dad L☺VES it!

He says I've gone to a ⟨LOT⟩ of trouble.

Actually it was Mum who put it on a T-shirt.

But I'm happy to take the praise.

Thank you. Thank you.

Dad wants to wear it straight away.

"IT FITS..." Mum says because she

thought it might be a bit snug.

(Which doesn't go down well with Dad.)

Derek says that **DOGZOMBIES** should have

T-shirts too. Which is an

EXCELLENT idea.

When Uncle Kevin, Aunty Alice and the cousins turn up, they are all wearing

VERY *fancy* clothes.

Dad wonders if they are going to another party afterwards?

Uncle Kevin says, "It's important to make an effort when you're invited out."

(He's looking at Dad like he's a bit scruffy.)

So Dad tells him that I made the T-shirt as a present.

"Tom's so talented, isn't it great?"

Which makes Delia do "I'm going to be sick" signs behind Dad's back.

I ignore her and AGREE with Dad, that I am a GENIUS ... it's true.

Uncle Kevin says, "Well done, Tom."

And Dad's happy ...

... until Aunty Alice gives him their present.

It's a book called

Uncle Kevin says,

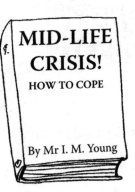

"We saw this and
thought of you."

Aunty Alice adds, "It was recommended for men of your age."

Dad says "Thanks!" but he doesn't look

THAT pleased.

THE FOSSILS arrive in their usual **STYLE**. Granny

cake

has brought one of her cakes
(well, I think it's a cake; you
never know with Granny).
I'm guessing Delia **FORGOT**
to buy Dad a present.
Because she's just given him ...
a pair of her **OLD**
sunglasses?

Dad puts them on and says, "Thanks, Delia, I look JUST like you now!"

Which is not really true
because Dad is SMILING.
Mum tells me I have to

look after Derek and
your cousins

(this means "keep out of trouble").

Everything's going well
until all the good snacks
run out.

Then the cousins announce that

they have brought over

so we can ALL finish watching it. ⊙ ⊙

"Let's watch it NOW,"
they say.
(Let's not.)

Derek looks keen to see it but I want to avoid
hiding behind cushions AGAIN.

QUICKLY I suggest, "We
should play a few jokes
instead."

Which turns out to be a BRILLIANT IDEA.

ha
ha

parp

The whoopee cushion

works well

on Delia.

And Aunty

Alice too.

parp

Putting me inside a LARGE box as an

"EXTRA present" for Dad was INSPIRED.

TO
DAD
xx

I SPRING out shouting

SURPRISE

Dad laughs but Uncle

Kevin's not smiling much,

because I've accidentally

knocked a bowl of crisps all over his
fancy bow tie.

Mum **AND** Uncle Kevin are GLARING at

me. **W**hen Granny comes to my rescue by
bringing in Dad's birthday cake.

...Which is slightly
unusual?

"It's a delicious
vegetable
cake," she says.

(Mmmm it doesn't look so delicious to me?)

We all sing "HAPPY BIRTHDAY"

to Dad.

(This is my version that I made up.)

"Happy birthday to you
You're a hundred and two
You've lost all your hair now
and your teeth are brand new!" ☺

Dad blows out his candles and calls me a
"cheeky monkey".

Uncle Kevin jokes that if we run out of
breath we might need a fire
extinguisher for all those candles.
Ha. Ha.

The cousins tuck into the cake
first. (No surprise there.)
It MUST taste better than it looks.

Then Granddad wants to REMIND us that

DOGZOMBIES are playing our

VERY *first* gig on Sunday...

WE ARE?

"This Sunday?

That's a bit soon, isn't it?" I say.

Granddad says it's all booked. So we'd better
get practising. Which is a good point because
we still only know a few songs.

"**B**esides, if you don't come and play, I'll be **FORCED** to entertain everyone with my ◯NE | VERY | special party trick," Granddad tells us.

Derek wants to know what

his *Party Trick* | actually | is.

(I'm not sure what it is either.)

Teeth

OK,

just remembered.

Meanwhile... The cousins ⎡STILL⎤ want
me to see the film. 👀
(I'd rather watch Granddad take his teeth out
again.) But it's too late, they are sitting in
front of the TV waiting for me to join them.

MYSTERIOUSLY ... the remote control
goes ⟨MISSING.⟩

(I've hidden it.)

I tell them that the TV is **STUCK**

Remote
control is
MISSING

on this channel. Which is showing a programme
on ... VAMPIRES. (That's lucky.)

I leave them to it. The cousins
are VERY happy until Aunty
Alice and Uncle Kevin come to take them home.

Which turns out to be a **lot** sooner

than expected due to Uncle Kevin

hurting his back. "I knew dancing was

a mistake," he says.

Dad says Uncle Kevin is (no spring chicken.

Not like the **FOSSILS,** who are

having a great time making everyone join in

their CONGA line. They dance all around the

house and into the garden too. It's slightly

embarrassing (but fun).

At least Dad looks like he's enjoying himself

this year.

Unlike Delia.

The Special ASSEMBLY

Get this...

Derek is off school today because he's sprained his ankle *doing that stupid conga.*

I have to go in on my own, which is FINE until I get to school and overhear Mr Keen talking to Mr Fullerman about the **SPECIAL ASSEMBLY.**

OH! NO! What with Dad's birthday and everything, I have completely forgotten all about the *special assembly* and playing in the school band!

(DEREK picked a good day for a dodgy ankle.)

I'm trying to avoid Mr Keen **AGAIN**, until
I can think of an | **EXCELLENT** |excuse to
get myself **OUT** of this sticky situation.
It's bad enough playing "instruments" (bottles
with chopsticks). But doing it without

Derek will be | too | embarrassing for me.

What to do?

I walk very *SLOWLY* into class to give
myself time to {think.}

Marcus is walking in front of me. He starts
LIMPING when he sees me.
"The dog bite scar?"
Marcus says. "It still hurts." This gives | me | an
idea. :)

(Thanks, Marcus, for a change.)

DISASTER! I am STRUCK

DOWN with a terrible   DEAD
ARM
ache...

Mr Fullerman wonders how this could have happened [SO] suddenly?

I explain how my older sister DELIA pushed me out of the house and how **she** MUST have sprained my "instrument-playing arm **VERY** badly".

"It's AGONY," I say.

I do some extra VERY LOUD groaning during registration, which I think helps. Mr Fullerman sends me to the medical room – again.

I moan a bit more (OK, a lot more, for extra effect on the way out).

Mrs Mumble tells me to sit in the medical room and wait for a bit.

Medical Room

UNFORTUNATELY

I miss **ALL** of the special assembly and playing in the school band too.
RESULT!

Once everything is safely over, I make a remarkable recovery.

My arm is fine now

... See.

Tah dah!

It's a MIRACLE.

It's safe to go back to class.

I just have to avoid Mr Keen for the rest of the day, which I manage to do with the help of:

Doors.

Walls.

And SOLID.

I can't avoid Mr Fullerman, though. He calls me over for a **"quick chat"**. (I think he's slightly suspicious about my instant recovery from arm ache.)

Mr Fullerman says,

"Such a shame you missed the special assembly, Tom."

(Not really.)

"Glad your arm is better ... so quickly, too?"

(Uh oh.)

I tell Mr Fullerman my arm feels absolutely FINE now. And THAT'S when I notice

the book under Mr Fullerman's arm.

IT's a book on TREES.

(Which looks VERY familiar?)

Mr Fullerman hands me back my

REViEW HOMEWORK.

The one I did so quickly.

About TREES...

It's all coming back

to me now ... whoops.

Tom

Imagine my surprise when I came
across this book on TREES ...
and realized I had read the back
somewhere before?

Your REVIEW HOMEWORK on trees,
Tom.

No more copying.

I want a new review done quickly
or another letter goes home to
your parents ... again.

Mr Fullerman

Point taken.

TREES:

This book aims to give you many interesting facts on trees. From where the largest tree in the world is, to how much food and shelter a tree can provide for wildlife.

Did you know that trees are the longest-living organisms on earth?

And that one acre of trees takes away nearly 2.6 tons of carbon dioxide each year?

The world's oldest trees are thought to be 4,600-year-old BRISTLECONE pines that are in the USA. There are so many benefits that trees bring to our cities and many communities. They provide beauty and shade. Trees can make you feel serene and peaceful.

I hope the information in this book will inspire you to enjoy trees and plant more of them.

By A. Corn

BAD NEWS ⚡☆

Mr Fullerman has REMOVED one of my GOLD STARS ☆ from my chart until I hand in the new piece of review homework. **"LAST CHANCE, Tom,"** he tells me. I can see that Marcus has a LOT more gold stars than I do. Which is annoying.

Mr Fullerman even gave him a gold star for **"collecting an unusual beetle".**

Which was REALLY irritating because I saw ⊙ ⊙ it first!

But he's WAY ahead of the whole class, even Amy. How's that happened?

Marcus is a sneaky so and so. Which makes me wonder if he's been

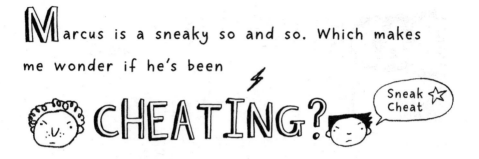

CHEATING?

Sneak ☆
Cheat

On the way home, I am discussing my suspicions about Marcus with Derek, who wants to get some fruit chews from the shop.

And guess who's already there?

→ 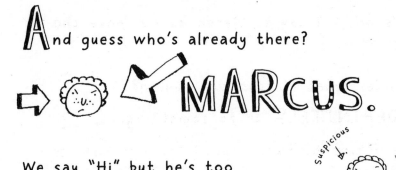 MARCUS.

We say "Hi" but he's too
busy looking for something ...
and it's NOT sweets.

Suspicious ↓

Gold star
stickers

Derek picks out a few fruit chews
while I read this week's
copy of **ROCK WEEKLY** (I'm off sweets
due to my dodgy tooth ... for now).

   When we leave the shop I notice that
MARCUS is standing in the section that
has paper, envelopes and ... stickers.

"That's odd," I say to Derek as we leave the shop.

"I wonder what Marcus was buying?"
He's DEFINITELY up to something.
So we decide to take a peek through the shop window.
Sure enough...
There's Marcus buying what looks like a very

LARGE box OF GOLD STAR STICKERS ☆☆☆☆☆

I knew it! Marcus has been adding his own stars to the chart. Catching him out won't be easy, though. I will need VERY BEADY EYES like Mr Fullerman's. ⊙ ⊙

DOGZOMBIES LAST BAND PRACTICE

Norman has come round for **DOG ZOMBIES** LAST band practice before our first gig. I tell him ALL about Marcus buying his own gold star stickers and CHEATING!

Norman thinks it's a GREAT IDEA!

(No, Norman, it's a bad idea ... sigh.)

We HAVE to learn ONE more song and practise the others.

Derek's dad keeps popping in and finding

excuses to come and see us rehearse.

Everything OK?

Even though we have ALL learnt

NOT to CHAT to Mr Fingle about music

(unless you have TEN HOURS ⊖ ⊖
to spare), right now we *NEED* his help.
Derek asks if he could suggest a good song for
us to learn ... today?

"Leave it to me, lads..."

(He's VERY excited.) He takes
out a Deep Purple record.

Another CLASSIC and perfect for you.

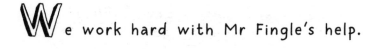

e work hard with Mr Fingle's help.

So **DOGZOMBIES** (that's us) have managed

to add

to our gig list.

RESULT!

Norman already knows how to play it and me

and Derek try our best. The singing is tricky,

especially when Mr Fingle keeps joining in.

Smoke on the water

Let's hope we've done enough to keep Granddad's teeth FIRMLY in his mouth on Sunday.

Now we've finished practising, Derek is looking for the last of the fruit chews he saved as a treat. But he can't find them anywhere. I haven't eaten them.

But I think I know who has...

It's a warning to us that

DOGZOMBIES FIRST-EVER GIG

YEAH!

BRILLIANT NEWS!

Delia's boyfriend ED has actually lent me

a REAL ELECTRIC guitar

and amp so I can play

REALLY LOUDLY!

From the look on Delia's face, it's all working fine.

ad says he's coming along as our

"ROADIE" to help set everything up. He's taking it all very seriously

(and he's made a long list).

DOGZOMBIES
banner ✓
BAND ✓
INSTRUMENTS ✓
POSTERS ✓
EARPLUGS ✓
DRINKS ✓

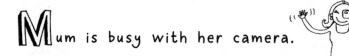

Mum is busy with her camera.

While we have our first BAND PHOTO done,

Dad keeps doing
embarrassing rock-star poses.

Me and **D**erek are a bit **nervous.**
Norman is always so jumpy that you can't
tell if he is or not.

I have a lucky escape when Mum tries to
HUG me and wishes the band
good luck.

Delia is her usual charming self.

You still here?

Dad has packed the car and stuffed the roof rack. Then we're off to meet Granddad. It's only when we're driving that I realize...

We have NO idea where exactly we're playing our first gig.

Dad says it will be a NICE BIG

SURPRISE...

for us!

"LEAFY GREEN OLD FOLKS' HOME ... ?" I say.

Granddad says they'll LOVE us.

"I have lots of friends here who are looking forward to seeing you!"

REALLY?

"And it won't matter how loud you play or if you make any mistakes because MOST of the audience are a bit hard of hearing. Just have some fun!"

Great. I'm wondering just how much "fun" the old folk are really going to have listening to us?

Pardon?

Granddad has put up LOTS of posters around the home already. He's now telling everyone that I'm his grandson and that **DOGZOMBIES** are going to be

THE NEXT BIG THING.

So they must come and see us.

(Thanks, Granddad.)

We have to wait for the lounge to be FREE before we can set up.

And I manage to avoid a potential disaster by keeping Norman away from the tray of biscuits. PHEW!

STEP AWAY!

We've got quite a crowd now, but it takes a while for the old folk to get settled and comfy.

When Granddad introduces us, he says,

"Can you all hear me back there?"
Which sets off everyone saying
"Pardon?" "Eh?" "Pardon?"
Never mind, we can play loudly.
Then Granddad says, "Let's give
a WARM LEAFY GREEN welcome
to the amazing ... **DOGZOMBIES**."

And it's over to us to start with a rousing edition of "Delia's a Weirdo" (which seems to all go down well).

The sign reads:

Tea and biscuits
(and band playing)
Today

Our first-ever gig was ... OK. Not brilliant ... just OK. (Room for improvement.) We made a few mistakes, but no one seemed to notice.

All in all, we had a good time, Norman didn't go too wild and Granddad's teeth stayed firmly in place the whole time, which is a good sign, I think? And I heard a few people singing "Delia's a WEIRDO" when we left. Result! ☺

 Granddad says there are a lot of other old folks' homes we could play. "Everyone has to start somewhere!" he reminds us.

True.

(I wonder where DUDE3 played their first gig?)

B ack at home I'm reading

D elia's copy of **ROCK WEEKLY**

and imagining that

DOGZOMBIES are being

interviewed by the magazine about the success

of their first-ever gig (and other important

music matters).

OLDIES ROCK OUT TO DOGZOMBIES' FIRST GIG!

Rock Weekly: So, Tom, who are your INFLUENCES for DOGZOMBIES?

Tom: That's a very good question. All sorts of things, really. DUDE3 are a huge influence. And I'm often inspired to write songs by VERY irritating family members.

RW: "Delia's a Weirdo"?

Tom: I couldn't have said it better myself...

RW: Why did you play your first gig at an old folks' home? It's an interesting choice.

Tom: Old folk like good music too. What can I say, we have a growing grey fan base who are spreading the DOGZOMBIE word!

RW: What's in the future for DOGZOMBIES?

Tom: World domination, I think, and a sponsorship deal with a delicious biscuit company would be nice?

Delia rudely interrupts me.

Are you pretending to be interviewed?

"No," I say unconvincingly.

You are! SADDO. ha! ha!

Then she takes back her copy of **ROCK WEEKLY** and goes off

LAUGHING!

Ha! Ha! Ha! Ha!

I think the next song I write will be called

"My Sister is an IDIOT".

I have lots of ideas already.

F resh from our SUCCESSFUL first-ever gig, me, Derek and Norman are reliving the WHOLE event in school.

I say, "There were loads of people all cheering and clapping."

Which is *SORT* of true. ☺

I don't mention it was at the LEAFY GREEN OLD FOLKS' HOME either.

In class, everyone is settling down when Mrs Mumble makes an announcement over the tannoy.

WILL TOM Gates and Norman Watson and Derek Fingle come to the school office TO See MR KEEN ...

Mr Fullerman is looking at me with his "what have you been up to **nOW?"** stare as we leave.

$\mathbb{D}$erek is already waiting outside the school office.

"What do you think Mr Keen wants?" he asks me.

"Who knows ... whatever it is, we're innocent," I say.

Norman's just happy to be out of lessons.

YEAH!

Turns out that Mr Keen has had a phone call from the owner of the LEAFY GREEN OLD FOLKS' HOME saying how impressed they were with the band. Apparently we're

I see ... yes.

"a credit to the school".

"Well done, all three of you,"
 Mr Keen says.

Then he goes and SPOILS

EVERYTHING by telling us,

"You'll be even better in the school band now!"

 Mr Sprocket is running a special
school band practice this lunchtime.

"I'll be showing some new parents around the school. It will be VERY impressive for them to see the band in action. Isn't that a good idea?"

(Eeeeeerrrrr, NO!)

NOT the school band again.

Mr Keen is DETERMINED to put us in the school band!

WHY? Looking at Derek I can see he's not wild about the idea. (Especially after last time.)

Norman doesn't seem to care because he's just spotted a spider walking up the wall.

I'm trying to think of YET another excuse to get OUT of this situation.
(Think! Mmmm ... mmmmm... Think! Mmmmmm...)
All kinds of ideas are going through my head.

Then it comes to me in a

F L A S H!

"Mr Keen," I say.

"Yes, Tom."
"Would you mind if we DIDN'T play in the school band? We were SO RUBBISH at playing the recycled instruments last time. It was terrible. Everyone thought so."

 "Oh … are you all sure?" Mr Keen asks.

"Very," I say.
Derek and Norman are nodding too.

PHEW! Look of relief

WHY didn't I think of saying that before?
And just like that, it's all sorted.
No more school band.

WRONG!

INSTEAD...

Mr Keen says that **DOG ZOMBIES** ♪♫

can play a special gig

in front of the

WHOLE ENTIRE

SCHOOL.

"Just like you did for the LEAFY GREEN OLD FOLKS' HOME.

So well done Tom for suggesting that," he adds.

(I didn't ... groan.)

On the way back to class I tell Derek and Norman it will all be fine because Mr Keen will probably forget about it. (He won't.)

"We're not ready to play in front of the school yet," I say.

We all agree on that.

Back in class.

I'm hoping Mr Fullerman might have heard the
news that Mr Keen was VERY pleased with
us (for a change). I might even get a bit of
PRAISE?
No, nothing yet. Oh well.

I get ready to join in the "class reading",
which is a nice and easy lesson.

I've even remembered to sneak a copy of
ROCK WEEKLY into my reading
book just in case things gets a bit dull.
(Emergency reading, I call it.)
    But Mr Fullerman says I'm EXCUSED from
class reading today because I still haven't given
in my REVIEW HOMEWORK.

"Have you, TOM?"

And if I don't finish it NOW I will
have to do it at lunch time in the library, with
Miss Page keeping an eye on me.

**"You don't want ANOTHER letter home,
do you, Tom?"**

"No, Mr Fullerman."
"And no copying books on trees."
Groan.
Marcus is sniggering next to me. He says, "No
gold stars for cheating", which is irritating.
OK. I'll do a REVIEW of DOGZOMBIES'
first gig. It's fresh in my memory and shouldn't
take long. I'll get it done before lunch.
I don't want to be stuck in the library, after
all.

In the library
I'm still finishing off
my homework.

I can hear people laughing and
PLAYING outside and the school band practising
in the hall. Miss Page is keeping
an EYE on me and a couple of
other kids too.

(At least I'm not in the school band any more
... that's something.)

I'm hoping this review homework will be worth
SIX MERITS and 3 gold stars

Because right now Marcus is STILL in the lead on the CHART. Although I'm convinced he's been

CHEATING, Cheat?

I can't prove it, which is annoying.

So I'm trying to get the last bit of my homework finished when I glance up and stare out of the window. I notice something a bit ODD.

From where I'm sitting in the library, I can see RIGHT INTO our CLASSROOM. SOMEONE is in there.

It doesn't look like Mr Fullerman, Mr Keen or any of the teachers.

I can't see who it is. So I keep watching.

I STAND UP

for a closer look.

Just when they duck down

under the desks.

Which is VERY suspicious.

The school band are still playing, so it can't be any of them (or Mr Sprocket).

Whoever it is has curly hair. I can see the top of their head moving closer

and closer

and closer

towards

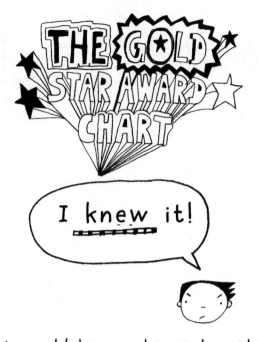

I knew it!

This could be my chance to catch
a very sneaky

CHEAT.

Smug

I ask Miss Page if I can leave.

Classroom ← All done

"Because Mr Fullerman
wants to check my
FINISHED REVIEW
HOMEWORK himself."
(Good thinking.)

Then I do super *FAST*
walking to get to the classroom.
I'm SO nearly there when I

BUMP

right into Mr Keen.
Who is busy showing
the new parents
around the school.

He asks me what I'm doing in school at lunch
time?
I say EXTRA studying
(which is sort of true).

Then Mr Keen tells the parents ALL about **DOGZOMBIES** and how we played at the

LEAFY GREEN OLD

FOLKS' HOME.

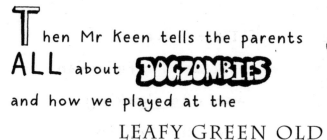

(He's going on a bit. Blah ... blah blah...)

I'm DESPERATE to get to the classroom!

Then just when I think he's finished chatting...

Mr Fullerman turns up!

And HE starts talking to the parents about **"the school field trip"** and what kind of work we do in class.

BLAH BLAH BLAH!

And ALL THE TIME

I'm thinking about who's in the

classroom ADDING the GOLD STARS to

the CHART !

When one of the PARENTS asks me,

What do YOU like
about your school,
Tom?

And THAT'S

when I get one of my TOTAL

BRAIN WAVES

I say...

"I really like the

GOLD STAR AWARD CHART

because it encourages you to do well in class."

(Superb answer.)

"Sounds interesting," they say.
                    "How does it work?"

 Mr Keen suggests I might like to show them in my classroom.

And I say, "That's an EXCELLENT idea, follow me."

Walking to the classroom I explain to the parents how we **EARN** merits for good work. And **TWO MERITS** equals

And the **ONLY** person who is allowed to give out the gold stars is **M**R FULLERMAN.

"You are DEFINITELY **NOT** allowed to stick the stars on yourself,

are you,

Mr Fullerman?"

I say.

"No, Tom, that's my job. And I hand out prizes at the end of term to whoever has the most gold stars."

We're nearly outside the classroom now.

So I say,

"If Mr Fullerman EVER caught someone adding their OWN stars ⭐ to the chart, that would be cheating, wouldn't it, Mr Fullerman?"

"Yes, Tom, it would be," he says.

Then I OPEN the classroom door, and just as I suspected...

There's Marcus Meldrew with a whole packet of his own gold stars.

(He's busted.)

Dear Mr and Mrs Meldrew

I am very disappointed to tell you that Marcus
has been caught adding his own stars to the
GOLD STAR AWARD CHART. In other words,
he's been caught cheating.

Marcus will be missing playtimes for the next
three days and helping Miss Page in the library
as a punishment.

Along with writing an apology letter to me.

I hope Marcus has learnt his lesson, as he is
capable of earning his own stars without
cheating.

Kind regards

Mr Fullerman

Class 5F Form Tutor

Due to Marcus CHEATING ...

his stars have been removed.

So now I'm *only* TWO STARS AWAY

from AMY PORTER (who's in the lead).

I need to get four merits (or more) for my

REVIEW HOMEWORK on the

DOGZOMBIES gig.

Mr Fullerman has been taking AGES

to mark my work.

When he does give it back to me he says

there's been a bit of a problem.

WHAT NOW?

Sorry, Tom.

I had a bit of an accident with my coffee!

Luckily it missed your homework and I was able to read and mark it finally.

Please make sure you do homework on time in future?

Mr Fullerman

DOGZOMBIES

FIRST-EVER GIG

REVIEW HOMEWORK AGAIN.

(For the ~~SECOND~~ THIRD TIME)

By Tom Gates.

If I was the lead singer of **DUDE3** I might be a tiny bit disappointed finding out the venue for the gig was THE LEAFY GREEN OLD FOLKS' HOME. But for **DOGZOMBIES'** first gig it was excellent.

My granddad **BOB** arranged it all (thanks, Granddad).

We had to carry a **LOT** of stuff into the home to set up.

Well ... when I say "WE", I mean my dad, who was our roadie for the day.

Before we could get started we had to wait for the

USE
IT OR
LOSE
IT
YOGA
CLASS

to finish.

Then Dad wasn't allowed to use the BIG hammer he brought to put up our

STOP!

DOGZOMBIES banner.

Luckily the surgical tape worked just as well.

SURGICAL
TAPE

G randdad said,

"Everyone who lives here is coming to see you because they are all

DOGZOMBIES FANS"

But I'm not so sure that's true. Because outside there was a sign that said tea and biscuits and band playing.

Tea and BISCUITS and band playing

I managed to **STOP** Norman from eating any biscuits before the gig started in case he went

WILD

(again).

It took a LONG time for everyone to get seated and comfortable.

And even l o n g e r for us to start playing.

This was mostly because:

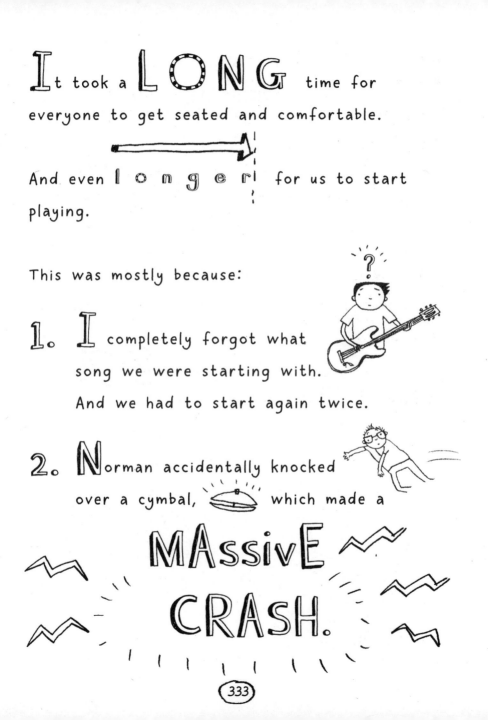

1. I completely forgot what song we were starting with. And we had to start again twice.

2. Norman accidentally knocked over a cymbal, which made a

MAssivE CRASH.

3. Some of the OLD FOLK got a BIT of a

SHOCK from the noise

and needed a top-up of tea and a biscuit

to calm down.

That's better.

4. Vera in the second row couldn't see

Vera

properly because Alfie's head

was in the way. So Dad had

to help Vera to a better seat.

5. Finally ... we were just about to get

started when FRED wanted to

know why we were called

DOGZOMBIES.

Which was a good question and took a bit of explaining.

EvENTuALLY ... we did

start playing. "Delia's a WEIRDO" went down well. So did " ".

But the best song of all was "SMOKE ON THE WATER".

Because everyone joined in by tapping the

sides of their teacups in time

with the music.

The whole **GIG** went SO well that at

the end we got a
STANDING OVATION...

Which is not easy to do

when the most of the audience

is well over

The End

Six merits, Tom, and
FOUR GOLD STARS.

WELL DONE!

Mr Fullerman

HOORAY!

Oh yes ... see those extra stars twinkling on the award chart!

Excellent!

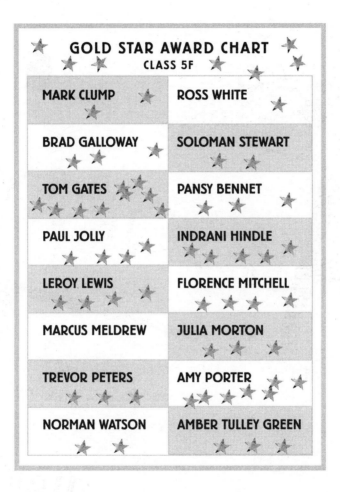

GOLD STAR AWARD CHART
CLASS 5F

MARK CLUMP	ROSS WHITE
BRAD GALLOWAY	SOLOMAN STEWART
TOM GATES	PANSY BENNET
PAUL JOLLY	INDRANI HINDLE
LEROY LEWIS	FLORENCE MITCHELL
MARCUS MELDREW	JULIA MORTON
TREVOR PETERS	AMY PORTER
NORMAN WATSON	AMBER TULLEY GREEN

What has **S**pots

Not many gold ☆ stars

(NOW)

And looks slightly less smug than usual

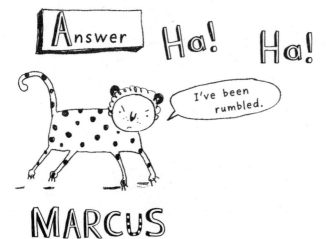

Answer Ha! Ha!

I've been rumbled.

MARCUS

(the cheater)

Finished reading
this book ALREADY?
You might like the same kind

of FUNNY stuff I do.
So check out my WEBSITE

www.scholastic.co.uk/tomgatesworld

Keep your BEADY EYES open for the other hilarious TOM GATES books!

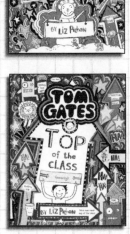

For more news about Liz Pichon and the Tom Gates books, go to: Lizpichon.com
AND to Scholastic's fantastic Tom Gates website: www.scholastic.co.uk/tomgatesworld

So many books

Good stuff

toom

I won a MASSIVE
pack of pens for coming (nearly)
TOP of the Gold Star Chart
AND a huge bar of chocolate
(eaten).

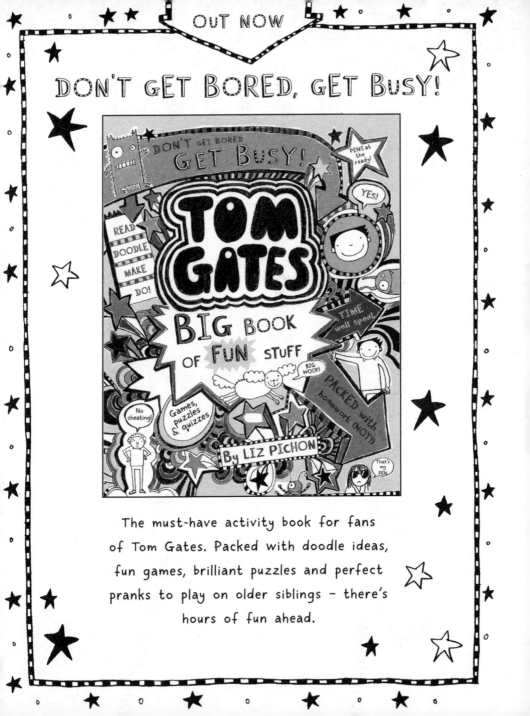

ONE VILE VILLAIN.
TWO VICIOUS DOGS.
THREE COURAGEOUS CHILDREN.

The flying shoes of your most EPIC dreams.

WELCOME TO SHOE TOWN.

Meet Ruby, Bear and Chelsea. They're RUNNING out of time to RESCUE their inventor dad from his HIDEOUS boss, WENDY WEDGE.

She'll do anything to win the glitzy GOLDEN SHOE AWARD and knows that entering flying shoes is her hot ticket to the trophy. Flying shoes that Ruby and Bear just HAPPEN to be hiding...

This can only mean one thing... it's SHOE WARS!

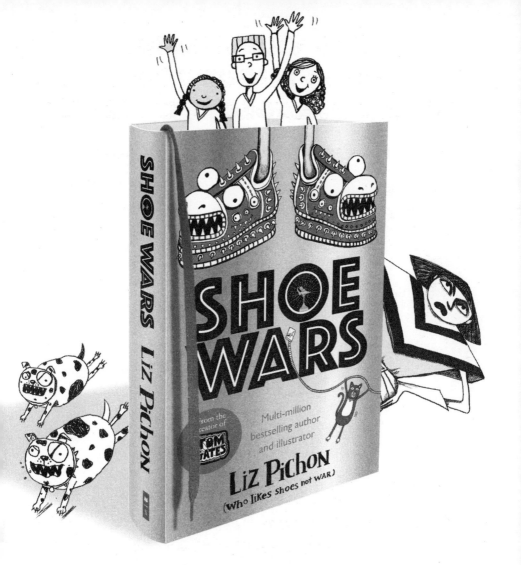

A laugh-out-loud, gadget-packed,
wedge-of-your-feet adventure like no other!

A *Sunday Times* children's book of the year.

"Full of Pichon's characteristic warmth, humour
and quirky illustrations" *The Bookseller*

Runners Up

Ava, 9, London

Oscar, 8, Todmorden

Laila, 14, London

Theo, 8, Gloucestershire

Stasha, 10, Indi

Josie, 8, Penarth

Ayaan, 9, Bromley

Ayaan, 9, Bromley

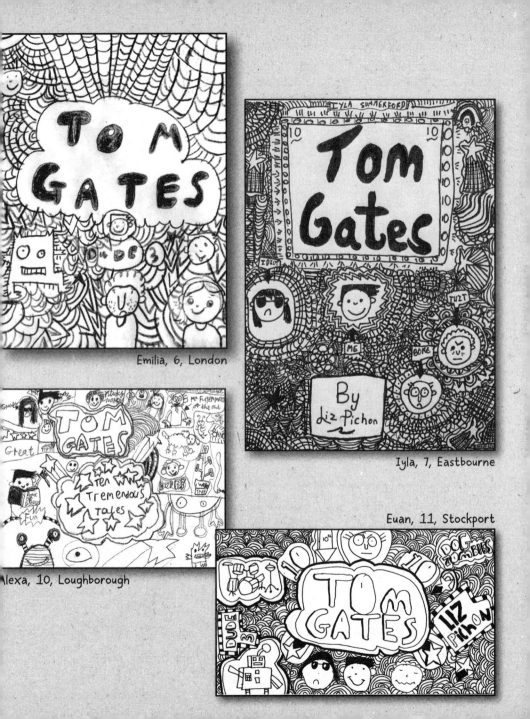

Emilia, 6, London

Iyla, 7, Eastbourne

Euan, 11, Stockport

Alexa, 10, Loughborough

River, 10, Falmouth

Annalie, 10, Woking

Lilly, 8, Eastbourne

Cayden, 11, Ferndale, Rhondda Cynon Ta

Ben, 10, Southampton

Jess, 12, Derbyshire

Inari, 13, Surrey

Wren, 6, Lancaster

Sebastian, 8, Telford

Isla, 9, Silverstone

Thomas, 8, Liverpool

Luca, 8, Eastbourne

Aurora, 10, Surrey

Camille, 9, Kent

Luca, 8, Eastbourne

Annie, 7, Shropshire

Sidra, 11, London

Harrison, 6, Hertfordshire

Evie, 12, Stockport

Joshua, 9, Middlesbrough

Oenone, 12, Bedfordshire

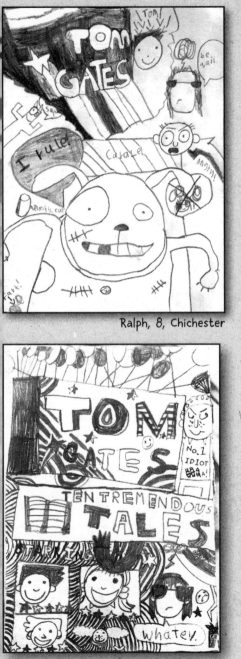

Ralph, 8, Chichester

Zackaria, 8, Edinburgh

Joseph, 9, Stockport

Ruari, 10, London

Leo, 7, Bristol

Joseph, 9, Tonbridge

Oliver, 7, Shoreham by Sea

Amira, 13, London

Stanley, 10, Leigh on Sea

Maya, 10, Grayshott

Jennifer, 12, Lincolnshire

Oscar, 9, Eastbourne

Joseph, 11, Balfron

Hammam, 11, Sale

Sara, 11, London

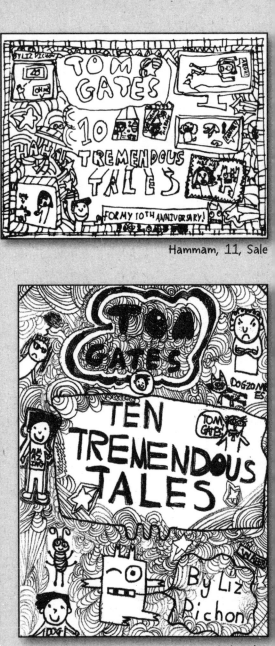

Lana, 9, London